RAVES FOR NEWBERY HONOR AUTHOR AND *NEW YORK TIMES* BEST SELLER JOAN BAUER!

★ "Via vivid characterizations, crisp, believable dialogue and some exciting scenarios, Bauer keeps her fans hooked for an entertaining ride."   —*Publishers Weekly*, starred review, on *Best Foot Forward*

★ "[Full of] fabulous and somewhat flamboyant characters, witty dialogue, and memorable scenes . . . Bauer's best yet."
—*SLJ*, starred review, on *Rules of the Road*

★ "Jubilant, strong, and funny, this is a road trip to remember."
–*BCCB*, starred review, on *Rules of the Road*

"An eloquent story of ordinary heroes."
—*Kirkus Reviews* on *Stand Tall*

"Rich with engaging characters, a light love interest, and dramatic tension in a well-paced plot, this is another great read from Bauer."
—*SLJ* on *Backwater*

"As always from Bauer, this novel is full of humor, starring a strong and idealistic protagonist, packed with funny lines, and peopled with interesting and quirky characters."
—*Kirkus Reviews* on *Hope Was Here*

★ "When it comes to creating strong, independent, and funny teenaged female characters, Bauer is in a class by herself."
–*SLJ*, starred review, Newbery Honor winner *Hope Was Here*

★ "This laugh-out-loud story is a delight."
—*SLJ*, starred review, on *Squashed*

★ "Fast-paced and engrossing entertainment that startles the reader with its underlying strength."
—*Publishers Weekly*, starred review, on *Squashed*

"Bauer's forcefully funny writing remains stylish from start to finish."
—*BCCB* on *Thwonk*

"Mickey's authentic voice draws readers right into the story."
—*Kirkus Reviews* on *Sticks*

Stay true to the story. . . .

It was Baker Polton!

"Are you all right?" I asked him.

"Depends on your definition of *all right*." He ripped up more of the newspaper, *The Albany Register*. "This used to be a great newspaper. I used to work at this paper. You know what it is now?" Tanisha picked up a shred. "Puff and puke." He sat back like he had a headache. He looked at me. "Why do you want to be a reporter?"

I thought for a second. "I care about the news and getting it right."

"Do something else. The field's changing too much. Don't get sucked in."

"But—"

"They're going to ask you to believe that entertainment is news. They're going to put things that don't matter on the front page and the ones that do on page twenty. They're going to tell you that flash and sex sell papers and that's all people are looking for these days. They're going to reduce your copy to sound bites and slogans and if they can figure out how to make a scratch-and-sniff midsized daily, believe me, they'll do it.

* * *

Home.

In my room. Laptop ready.

I sent the e-mail, short and sweet.

Mr. Polton,

How do you stand up for truth?

Peeled

✿✿✿✿✿✿✿✿✿✿✿✿✿✿✿✿✿✿✿✿✿✿✿✿✿✿✿

JOAN BAUER

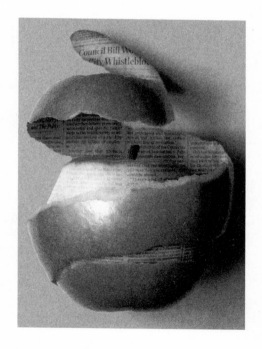

speak

An Imprint of Penguin Group (USA) Inc.

This book is for my mother,
Marjorie Good,
whose hope, faith, and grace inspire me every day.

SPEAK
Published by the Penguin Group
Penguin Group (USA) Inc., 345 Hudson Street, New York, New York 10014, U.S.A.
Penguin Group (Canada), 90 Eglinton Avenue East, Suite 700, Toronto, Ontario, Canada M4P 2Y3
(a division of Pearson Penguin Canada Inc.)
Penguin Books Ltd, 80 Strand, London WC2R 0RL, England
Penguin Ireland, 25 St Stephen's Green, Dublin 2, Ireland (a division of Penguin Books Ltd)
Penguin Group (Australia), 250 Camberwell Road, Camberwell, Victoria 3124, Australia
(a division of Pearson Australia Group Pty Ltd)
Penguin Books India Pvt Ltd, 11 Community Centre, Panchsheel Park, New Delhi - 110 017, India
Penguin Group (NZ), 67 Apollo Drive, Rosedale, North Shore 0632, New Zealand
(a division of Pearson New Zealand Ltd.)
Penguin Books (South Africa) (Pty) Ltd, 24 Sturdee Avenue, Rosebank, Johannesburg 2196, South Africa

Registered Offices: Penguin Books Ltd, 80 Strand, London WC2R 0RL, England

First published in the United States of America by G. P. Putnam's Sons,
a division of Penguin Young Readers Group, 2008

Published by Speak, an imprint of Penguin Group (USA) Inc., 2009

1 3 5 7 9 10 8 6 4 2

THE LIBRARY OF CONGRESS HAS CATALOGED THE G. P. PUTNAM'S SONS EDITION AS FOLLOWS:
Bauer, Joan, date.
Peeled/Joan Bauer. p. cm.
Summary: In an upstate New York farming community, high school reporter Hildy Biddle
investigates a series of strange occurrences at a house rumored to be haunted.
ISBN: 978-0-399-23475-0 (hc)
[1. Reporters and reporting—Fiction. 2. Journalism—Fiction. 3. Farm life—New York (State)—Fiction.
4. Haunted houses—Fiction. 5. High schools—Fiction. 6. Schools—Fiction.
7. New York (States)—Fiction.] I. Title.
PZ7.B32615Pee 2008 [Fic]—dc22
2007042835
Speak ISBN 978-0-14-241430-9

Printed in the United States of America

Design by Marikka Tamura
Text set in Janson

"In the age of information overload, newspapers must be the medium that people believe. They don't have to be first. They can even be last. *But they must be right.*"

—Pete Hamill, *News Is a Verb*

Chapter 1

✾✾✾✾✾✾✾✾✾✾✾✾✾✾✾✾✾✾✾✾✾✾✾✾✾✾✾✾✾✾✾✾✾✾✾✾✾✾

DATELINE: Banesville, New York. May 3.

Bonnie Sue Bomgartner, Banesville's soon-to-be 67th Apple Blossom Queen, let loose a stream of projectile vomiting in the high school cafeteria.

"It was the tuna fish," she gasped miserably, and proceeded to upchuck again.

I wrote that down on my notepad as Darrell Jennings and I took a big step back.

The crowning of the queen was tomorrow at 10:00 A.M. in the Happy Apple Tent—a major moment in my small town of Banesville, an orchard-growing community in Upstate New York where apples are our livelihood and the core of our existence.

The nurse rushed in. Darrell, the editor of *The Core*, the high school paper where I worked as a reporter, said, "It's a cliffhanger, Hildy. The festival law says if the queen is sick and can't appear, the runner-up gets crowned."

"I didn't know that."

He pushed his glasses onto his head and grinned. "That's why I'm the editor."

I jabbed him in the arm for that comment. Darrell has been editing my copy for close to forever.

Bonnie Sue heaved again and the nurse mentioned something about food poisoning.

"My brother had food poisoning and it kept coming up all weekend," Darrell whispered ominously. "Stay on this, Hildy. This could be big. Bigger than big. I want the story behind the story."

He always says that.

Mrs. Perth, the festival coordinator, who also worked in the school office, ran in. "She'll be fine, everyone."

Bonnie Sue looked close to apple green. I felt for her, honestly, even though she was the kind of gorgeous girl who acted like she was personally responsible for her looks.

Mrs. Perth handed Bonnie Sue a tub of lip gloss. Bonnie Sue glossed and stuck her head back in the bucket.

"*Everything*," Mrs. Perth said fiercely, "will be *fine*."

She shooed us out of the cafeteria, but not before she said to me, "Hildy, of course we don't want to mention this incident in our paper."

I looked at my notes. "Why not?"

"Hildy, the Apple Blossom Festival is about the hope of the harvest yet to come."

Banesville needed a good harvest. We were still reeling

from two bad harvests in a row. This was a make-or-break year for the orchards.

"I understand about the hope, Mrs. Perth, but a queen with food poisoning is kind of interesting and—"

Mrs. Perth forced out a smile. "The Apple Blossom Queen is the symbol of unbridled joy and farm-fresh produce." Her plump hand covered mine. "And we wouldn't want that symbol to be tarnished in any way. Would we?"

"But Bonnie Sue has food poisoning. That's the truth."

"The *truth*," she snarled, "is that we've had quite enough problems in Banesville! This festival is committed to being happy and positive from beginning to end!" Her eyes turned to slits. "You're *just* like your father, Hildy Biddle."

"Thank you," I said quietly. She shut the cafeteria door in my face.

From behind the door, I heard Bonnie Sue bellow, *"I'm not giving up my crown! I earned it! It's mine!"*

I wrote that down, too.

I was standing in front of Frankie's Funny Fun Mirrors, watching them stretch my legs and elongate my neck and head as the Apple Blossom Festival pulsated around me.

Two little boys ran up, snickering.

"What's worse than finding a worm in an apple you're eating?" the bigger one asked me.

"What?"

3

"Finding half a worm!"

They grabbed their throats, shrieked, "Eeeewwww!" and ran off.

I made a face in the mirror, stuck out my tongue.

Hildy Biddle, reporter at large.

I headed across the midway that was actually Banesville High's football field. I walked under the great arch of blossoms, passing men dressed like Johnny Appleseed. I turned left at the storytelling tent where Granny Smith, our local storyteller, was holding forth; did a twirl and a two-step past Bad Apple Bob and the Orchard Boys playing their foot-stomping regional hit, "You Dropped Me Like an Apple Peel on the Ground."

"Oh, baby," I sang along with them, "why'd you have to go?"

You're just like your father, Hildy Biddle.

I guess that meant obstinate, unbending, always searching for truth.

I can live with that.

I remembered being with Dad at the festival when I was little, riding the Haunted Cider Mill roller coaster, hiding behind him when the wicked queen from *Snow White* walked by with her poisoned apple. We'd eat fat caramel apples, drink cider till our stomachs would groan. Everywhere I looked, there seemed to be a memory of him.

He died three years ago from a heart attack.

I still can't imagine what God was thinking when he let that happen.

I looked up in the sky and saw Luss Lustrom's two-seater prop plane flying overhead. I waved even though he couldn't see me. Luss gave air tours of the apple valley. I rode with him last year. I'll never forget the experience—flying low over the apple trees that were in full blossom. The sky seemed bluer than it did when I was standing on the ground; the valley seemed sweeter; the promise of good soil that people would fight for and cry over seemed real to me.

Luss did his best cackling ghost laugh as we flew over the old Ludlow property, a place some people in town thought was haunted.

"The ghost of old man Ludlow," Luss shouted darkly. "Will we see him?"

I hoped not.

I had wanted to keep flying in the sky with Luss and not come down, but when your family owns an orchard, coming down to earth isn't optional.

I headed to the Happy Apple Tent, where the queen would be crowned. Bonnie Sue Bomgartner wasn't anywhere to be seen. She had missed the filling of the giant grinning apple balloon. She'd missed Mayor Frank T. Fudd's annual declaration: "I can feel it in my bones; this is going to be the best festival ever!" The tent was crammed with people. Tanisha Bass, my best friend and *The Core*'s photographer, was stationed by the entrance. A group of small children dressed like honeybees held hands and wove through the crowd.

My cousin Elizabeth, *The Core*'s graphic artist, who wrote for the paper *only* when we were desperate for copy, whispered, "I heard Bonnie Sue is still at home."

Darrell, our editor, shook his head. "She made it to the convertible in her pink dress."

"And puked on the dress, I heard." That was Lev Radner, my second former boyfriend and *The Core*'s marketing manager.

I looked at Lev's thick, curly dark hair, his blue eyes, his chiseled jaw. He was seriously cute, but I'm sorry, when a guy cheats on me—and this does happen with disturbing regularity—I'm gone.

T. R. Dobbs, our sportswriter, marched up. "This just in—the convertible turned back."

"How do you know this?" I demanded.

"I never divulge my sources," T.R. said, smiling.

"Big woman approaching." Tanisha pointed to Mrs. Perth, who was chugging toward the tent, apple blossoms bouncing on her straw hat, not a happy camper.

I stepped into her path. "Mrs. Perth, could you—"

She almost ran me over! *"Are you coming?"* she barked, looking behind her.

I looked to see Lacey Horton, the Apple Blossom Queen runner-up, walking hesitantly toward the tent, not in the traditional pink dress with pink heels, but in jeans, boots, and a work shirt. Lacey was president of the Horticulture Club and, like me, the child of family orchard owners.

She caught up with Mrs. Perth, who snapped, "How you think you can represent the growers of Banesville dressed like that, Miss Horton, I will never know."

Lacey smiled sweetly. "All I know how to be is myself."

Mrs. Perth harrumphed and handed Lacey a tub of lip gloss. Lacey handed it back.

I took notes like mad. Tanisha snapped shots. Suddenly another photographer elbowed his way past Tanisha and started photographing Lacey.

Tanisha tapped him on the shoulder. "Excuse me."

The guy ignored her. His cap read *Catch the buzz in Banesville . . . Read* THE BEE. *The Bee* is our local newspaper.

Mrs. Perth hissed, "Let's get this over with."

Lacey looked down. She wasn't gorgeous like Bonnie Sue, but she was pretty enough, with dark brown hair and green eyes.

"Congratulations, Lacey," I said, grinning. "How's it feel to be queen?"

"Weird," she whispered.

"We've had so many challenges in town," I continued. "What's it mean to you to be queen of this year's festival?"

Mrs. Perth interrupted, "We don't have time for—"

"I'd like to answer Hildy's question, Mrs. Perth." Lacey smiled at me. "It means that maybe I can help people understand what it's like to be a small farmer."

I felt like cheering.

Lacey wasted no time redefining her role. She stood on the stage, one hand steadying her crown, the other holding the microphone.

"We all know in Banesville how things can change suddenly, like the weather," she began.

People chuckled. That was for sure.

"I know that lots of you have come from out of town—we welcome you to Banesville and hope you have a wonderful time at our festival. I'd like to say something to all the people who are growers in this area." She looked around the packed tent. "It's been a hard two years; my family and I know that firsthand. Lots of us have suffered, the bad weather has hurt our crops. But I know how much every grower loves their land. That's why we're still here, still able to celebrate the hope of a new harvest. I'm so proud to be a part of this!" She turned grinning to her parents, who were beaming in the front row.

"We can't give up," Lacey continued. "We need to stand together. So today, let's celebrate the hard work, the good land, and the wonderful produce that come from it."

The crowd burst into applause. Tanisha's little white dog, Pookie, ran across the stage in a sequined pink sweatshirt and jumped into Lacey's arms. Pookie is the unofficial mascot of Banesville.

A huge roar of approval went up.

A little girl tugged at my shirt. "Is she a farmer or a queen?"

"Both," I said, smiling.

"Cool!"

Yes. Very cool.

I titled my article on Lacey "Long Live the Queen!" I included the behind-the-scenes vomiting drama, written sensitively, of course. I tried to interview Bonnie Sue Bomgartner to see how she was doing, having lost the crown and all, but she told me to take a walk in dog poop and mind my own business. It was one of the best pieces I'd written for the paper.

I'd officially broken free now from the early days of high school journalism, with groaner topics like "Hooray for Health Week" and "Locker Safety for Dummies."

But I wanted to take on more.

All summer long, I read every piece of fine reporting I could get my hands on. I practiced writing lead sentences and drove my family and friends crazy asking the questions all reporters have to ask to get to the meat of a story—*who, what, where, when, why,* and *how*.

By July, my grandmother Nan would head the other way when she saw me coming. "Hildy Biddle," she'd shout, "I swear, if you ask me one more time what I'm doing, where I'm going, why I'm going, when I'm coming back, who I'm meeting with, and how I'm feeling about the world, I'm going to start screaming and not stop!"

Asking questions is an art, but not everyone appreciates the beauty.

I kept asking questions all summer as the spooky signs began to appear on the front door of the old Ludlow house.

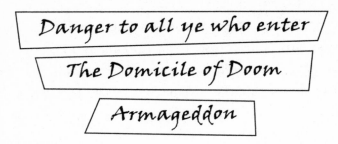

Danger to all ye who enter

The Domicile of Doom

Armageddon

"Who's putting those signs up?" I asked. No one in town knew.

"What should be done?" I demanded.

"Why isn't someone tearing them down?"

When people have had a few bad years, they tend to let things go.

A few weird-looking characters were coming to town, too. One woman I saw had a shaved head and was wearing skeleton earrings. The guy she was with had a deathly white face.

"Where's the ghost house?" they asked drearily.

"Up on the hill," I told them.

Then, in August the high school auditorium roof collapsed without warning. School hadn't started yet, thank God; no one was hurt.

It felt like something bad was seeping into the atmosphere—until, that is, you looked at our fields, which were finally bringing forth an abundant harvest. It's hard to think dark thoughts when you're biting into a juicy peach, tough to focus on ghostly gloom when you're gobbling sweet corn slathered with salted butter and finishing the meal off with blueberry shortcake with mounds of fresh whipped cream. By late August the tables at the Banesville Farmers Market were heavy with heirloom tomatoes, sweet nectarines, heavenly plums, summer squash, and peppers. The early apples were rolling off the trucks—crisp, sweet, and filled with the promise that so much more was coming.

There were a few stories in *The Bee* about the Ludlow place and how there'd been ghost sightings. Some unnamed businessperson who claimed to have seen old man Ludlow's ghost was quoted: "I think Banesville better brace itself for trouble."

"Do you think that place is haunted?" Tanisha asked me.

I wasn't sure. I just wanted that house to go away.

Everyone was talking about it.

My father always told me, "When a story keeps coming at you day and night, pay attention." Dad was a reporter, too.

The phone call came in early September.

I'm here to tell you, I paid attention.

Chapter 2

DATELINE: September 9. Banesville, New York.

I fumbled for the ringing phone.

"Hildy." It was Darrell Jennings. "Look, I know it's early."

It took a minute for my eyes to focus on the alarm clock: 5:23 A.M. "It's extremely early, Darrell; it's inappropriately early—"

"Not when you hear what happened."

"What?" I pulled my comforter higher.

"There was an attempted break-in at the Ludlow house, the guy's in jail, and there's another sign."

I was sitting up now, fumbling for the light.

"I want you on this, Hildy. This is a big, emerging story. And need I mention how much *The Core* needs a big, emerging story . . . ?"

All last year *The Core* had been struggling for advertisers, struggling for readership.

"You're the best reporter," Darrell half cooed.

I sighed. Flattery has power.

"The sheriff is at the Ludlow house," he added. "Neighbors have gathered outside, and the house just made the top-ten list of most haunted places in Upstate New York."

"I heard about the list yesterday." I was looking for my shoes. "How do you know about the break-in?" I asked, and then I remembered. Last week Darrell bought a police radio receiver on closeout, vowing that high school journalism at Banesville High would never be the same.

"I called Tanisha, Hildy. She's got her camera and is coming to pick you up."

"*When* is she coming?" I demanded.

"In ten minutes."

"I can't believe this!"

"Ask tons of questions, Hildy, and be unendingly pushy. You're great at that."

I know.

A siren in the distance; a hand-scrawled sign.

> *You Didn't Think It Was Safe,*
> *Did You?*

It hung from the torn screen door of the old Ludlow place. Dawn was just beginning. A tangerine glow inched across the dark sky. I wrote the message down on my notepad.

Tanisha, a committed morning person, said, "Are we scared yet?"

"Nervous, possibly."

She studied me. "You got dressed fast."

"Right."

"Really fast." She pointed at my shoes. I was wearing one black and one tan sandal.

I groaned as Tanisha snapped shots of the house. She always looked put together—her jeans fit perfectly, her red shirt slimmed at the waist, her boots weren't scuffed.

But a reporter can't let bad footwear stop her.

I marched to the rusty front gate.

Details, I thought. Get the details.

I wrote,

garbage inside fence

dilapidated porch swing creaking

iron fence rusted, paint peeling, porch missing steps

clusters of neighbors on street

Sheriff Metcalf was putting up yellow tape around the fence that read, POLICE LINE—DO NOT CROSS. I walked over to him.

"Hi, Sheriff."

"What are you doing here, Hildy?"

Not everyone is glad to see you when you're a reporter. "I'm covering this for *The Core*."

"Good God," he muttered.

"I understand there was a break-in, Sheriff. Could you tell me—"

"We'll be issuing a statement." He looked up and down the street and shouted, "Nothing to see here, folks. We've got everything under control."

"Were things out of control?" I asked him.

"We'll be issuing a statement."

I wrote, *"we'll be issuing a statement"* x 2—*sheriff crabby.*

"If you ask me," a man said behind me, "old man Ludlow's ghost is making his presence known."

I turned to him. "Why do you say that, sir?"

"You got two mysterious deaths that happened here thirty years ago. Everyone figures the old man did it, even though he was never convicted. The ghosts in this place aren't happy, not one bit."

"Don't forget poor little Sallie Miner," a woman in a bathrobe added.

Five years ago, Sallie Miner, a local girl, was riding her bike in front of this house. A tree branch crashed in front of her and hurled her into the street in front of an SUV that couldn't stop in time. Sallie died three days later. But before she died, she told people what she'd seen when the tree branch fell—the ghostly face of an old man laughing in the Ludlow house window.

No one was living there at the time, either.

The house had been abandoned for years, although it was owned by old man Ludlow's sister. She didn't do anything to maintain it. Garbage bags lay on the lawn next to Styrofoam cups, beer cans, banana peels.

"People are coming here at night to see the ghost and leaving their refuse," Pinky Sandusky, a Farnsworth Road neighbor, complained to me. "This place is becoming a circus. We need to stop this before it gets worse."

"Have you ever seen any signs of a ghost?" I asked her. Pinky was a friend of Nan's.

"There's places on the street that are hot and cold," she mentioned. "That's a sure sign."

"A sure sign of what?"

"Menopause," a middle-aged woman joked, and a few older women laughed.

I wrote, *menopause—hot and cold.*

"It's a sure sign of a ghostly presence," Pinky asserted. "I've lived in Banesville for seventy-three years. Things are changing and not for the better!"

Tanisha was sneaking around, taking photos of the people. She stood on a tree stump, climbed up on her car hood.

It was then that Pen Piedmont, the editor and publisher of *The Bee*, our local newspaper, strutted onto the scene, thumbs in his suspenders, slicked-back hair gleaming. He sauntered up, looking briefly at my mismatched sandals.

"Big goings-on, folks." He had a game show host's voice. "How are you dealing with this growing menace?"

"Ever since those signs appeared, I can't sleep at night."

"I'm calling the mayor—something needs to be done!"

"Some of the folks congregating here are scaring my kids."

"That house of horrors is going to bring this town down!"

Piedmont didn't take any notes as people talked. I was writing so much, I was almost out of paper. A man said that at 5:00 A.M. he'd heard men's voices on the property and called the police.

"And one man was arrested?" I asked him.

He shook his head. "The sheriff's not talking."

I'd noticed that.

"This isn't helping property values," Mr. Hardine, another neighbor, snarled. He looked next door to his freshly painted blue house; a FOR SALE sign was on the lawn. "You think people are going to want to buy a place next to all *that*?"

A tap on my shoulder. I turned to see Eaton Ebbers. He's close to a legend in Banesville, having gone eight full days on *Jeopardy!*

"I've lived on this street for fifty-nine years," he told me. "And I'll tell you something. Fear changes people."

I studied the collection of neighbors surrounding Pen Piedmont, giving him an earful. The new sign on the Ludlow front door was hard to ignore: *You Didn't Think It Was Safe, Did You?*

Eaton Ebbers shook his gray head. "When people are scared, they look for something to blame."

I turned to him. "I'm not sure I understand."

"You will," he said, and walked away.

Banesville High.

Room 67B. *The Core*'s official office, although "office" was pushing it; "windowless closet" came closer. I did an Internet search and found the website for Top Haunted Houses in Upstate New York.

CLICK here for our bloodcurdling scream audio.

I'll pass, thanks.

The Top Ten Most Haunted list was front and center. I pressed print; the paper whirred out.

WANT TO GET SCARED?

Haunted Houses in Upstate New York has just announced our top ten spookiest places, guaranteed to send thrills and chills up your spine. While many old favorites still dominate the list, we welcome a newcomer, Banesville's old Ludlow house, ranked #6 in "fright, foreboding, and foul play." The house was the site of a double murder thirty years ago and has been unnerving this sleepy apple valley hamlet ever since.

People say that old man Ludlow was a jealous man, obsessed with his young, beautiful wife and thoughts that she might leave him. And she may

18

have tried to—she and her boyfriend were found asphyxiated in the garage, with packed suitcases in the car; the garage doors had been locked from the outside. The old man was questioned for years about the deaths but never convicted. The deaths were labeled an accident. Ludlow dismantled the freestanding garage, planted apple trees over the spot, and grew steadily crazier, never again leaving his property and only coming outside at night. Eventually he was found dead by the grove of apple trees and now haunts the property, seeking to kill again. "We got something living there, no doubt," said one lifelong resident. "It ain't too keen on company, I can promise you that."

**For bus tours of our ten top haunts, please call early for reservations.

I was sitting at the desk along the wall. The VERITAS sign hung crooked in front of me—*veritas* is the Latin word for "truth." I grabbed some Doritos from the food heap as Royko, this week's fly, buzzed overhead—he was named for Mike Royko, a Chicago columnist who won the Pulitzer Prize. Last spring we had an ant named Mencken, named for H. L. Mencken, a famous journalist of the forties. We try our best to honor the greats.

My mess of notes spread before me, I typed, *An early morning break-in at the old Ludlow house on Farnsworth Road was stopped Friday when a neighbor heard voices on the property and called the sheriff's office. Sheriff Metcalf said he would be issuing a statement about the incident; it appears that at least one man was arrested.*

I checked my notes. What else did I know for sure?

On Thursday, the house was named #6 on the Internet site Top Ten Haunted Houses in Upstate New York. Ghost stories about the house and Mr. Ludlow are not new, but concern in town is growing as strangers begin to congregate at the Ludlow property, disturbing the neighborhood and frightening the children.

How do I put this?

Many neighbors wonder about the safety of the house; some say they have heard ghostly noises. Others expressed concern about declining property values on Farnsworth Road. Words of wisdom and caution came from our own Jeopardy! *master, Eaton Ebbers, a Farnsworth Road resident: "Fear changes people," he said. "When people are scared, they look for something to blame."*

Not bad for a start. Of course, I needed more, like who was arrested. If the sheriff wouldn't talk to me, how could I find that out?

It would have helped if we'd had an adviser. Mr. Loring, our beloved adviser, took early retirement last June and moved to Florida.

How he could leave us, I'll never know.

Darrell stomped in, enveloped by journalistic passion. "This just in, Hildy. The man arrested in the break-in is going before Judge Forrester today at two o'clock."

20

Darrell checked the chart on the wall where he'd taped the staff's class schedules.

"Perfect. You have a study hall from 1:50 to 2:45 today," he noted. "Are we on top of this or what?" Darrell looked at me with emotion as the overhead fluorescent light flickered. "I want the story behind the story. So get over to the courthouse and let them know who we are!"

"The bold voice of Banesville High," I mumbled.

Darrell jabbed the air as Royko buzzed around his head.

Chapter 3

❖❖❖❖❖❖❖❖❖❖❖❖❖❖❖❖❖❖❖❖❖❖❖❖❖❖❖❖❖❖❖❖❖❖❖❖❖❖❖

I'd never been in a courtroom before. A man in a brown suit sat at one of two tables in front of the judge's elevated desk. I had no idea what to do, but jumping in with both feet is one of my endearing qualities.

"Excuse me," I said to the man. "Are you here about the attempted break-in at the Ludlow house? I'm supposed to cover this for my high school newspaper."

"I'm waiting for the judge," he said dismissively.

Nobody takes teenage reporters seriously.

A uniformed man walked into the courtroom and announced, "All rise."

Judge Forrester walked in, looking stern. He was the father of Nathan Forrester, my first former boyfriend, who cheated on me with Leandra Penn.

I waved at the judge and he looked surprised to see me. I found a seat in the back, and whipped out my notepad.

A middle-aged man wearing black pants, a black shirt, and sneakers was brought in.

The uniformed man told the judge this was the defendant, Houston Bule.

Great name. I wrote that down.

"Mr. Bule," Judge Forrester began, "can you tell me why you were on the Ludlow property at five o'clock this morning?"

Bule said, "I was there working security."

"For whom?"

The man in the brown suit stood. "Your Honor, my client works part-time for D&B Security."

Judge Forrester interrupted. "I'd like Mr. Bule to tell me his story."

"I was brought in by D&B," Bule explained. "People had been trespassing on the property. We were looking to see how to make the house safer. That's all I know."

"Now, I'm just a simple country judge, Mr. Bule, but explain to me why that needed to be done *at five o'clock in the morning.*"

"That's when they told me to do it."

Judge Forrester looked at some papers. "The arresting deputy's report, Mr. Bule, said you were trying to pick the lock at the Ludlow kitchen door. Why would you do that, sir?"

"I forgot the keys."

"I see. And who told you to pick the lock?"

"The boss, Donny Lupo. He said Martin would be mad if we didn't do the job."

"Who's Martin?"

"No idea."

Judge Forrester pressed on. "Where is Mr. Lupo now, Mr. Bule?"

"I don't know. I went one way; Donny went the other."

The man in the brown suit stood again. "Your Honor, D&B Security is a bonded—"

The judge raised his hand for silence. "Your client has three prior breaking-and-entering convictions. Until we locate Mr. Lupo, we'll keep Mr. Bule safe and well-fed in our county jail."

"Your Honor, I propose under the circumstances that bail be set."

"Picking a lock is a serious offense in this county. *Remand*." Judge Forrester slammed his gavel down.

I can see why Nathan twitched whenever his father came in the room.

I wrote, *what's remand?*

Bule was led away. The man in the brown suit marched past me out the double doors.

I walked out of the courtroom, too. I stopped at the front desk and asked the woman behind it, "What does *remand* mean?"

"Held in custody until the next court appearance," she explained.

"Cool." I wrote that down, then looked up at the town banner hanging on the wall.

BANESVILLE, NEW YORK
The Happiest Town in the Happy Apple Valley

Uh . . . *not* quite . . .

When I got home, I added the new information to my article.

The alleged intruder, Houston Bule, was arrested and is being held without bail in the county courthouse while another man—

A knock on my bedroom door. My cousin Elizabeth came in carrying a yellow smiley-face candle. We've lived together for three years, ever since Mom and I moved here after Dad died. Her blond hair was pulled back in a tight ponytail. She has a pretty, heart-shaped face.

"Nan says we have to come down now." It was Friday night—our family's big push to get ready for the Saturday farmers market. Elizabeth put the smiley-face candle on my desk.

"I think the entire Ludlow thing is beyond creepy, Hildy, and I think we should all light candles or something, you know, to dispel the darkness." She lit the candle; the flame illuminated the happy face. She put a card next to it that read:

25

Little candle burning bright
Bring your light into this night.

"I'm praying you'll be okay writing about the ghost," she said.

I smiled. "So far it's working."

"I don't think you realize, Hildy, that Darrell gave you this assignment because he knows you're the only one who can handle it." She plopped on my bed, exuding sweetness. It wasn't fake, either, although I admit, when we first started living together, I didn't think she was for real. Nan said Elizabeth was like God's little flower blooming in a land of weeds.

This begged a question.

"Am I a weed?" I asked Nan.

"You're a flower, too, Hildy."

"Which one?" I hoped she wasn't going to say a snapdragon.

Nan pointed out the window to her garden, a gift to the neighborhood. "Why, you're a rose, darlin'. You've got a few prickly parts, but they're nothing compared to the beauty you put out."

I could live with that.

Elizabeth hugged the bed pillow she'd made me that read, NEVER, NEVER GIVE UP. "You don't ever seem afraid, Hildy."

That surprised me. "I'm scared lots of times. I guess I don't like to show it."

"I think you're brave."

"Well, thanks."

Elizabeth is brave, too, but in less obvious ways. Her mom died when she was a baby, and she and her dad, Felix, are a lot like cheese and chocolate—it's hard to imagine them blending together. I mentioned this to her once, but Elizabeth found the exception. She made dinner that night—chicken with melted cheese and Mexican mole sauce, a kind of chocolate gravy. Nan, Mom, and I loved it. Uncle Felix had fourths.

"We'd better get downstairs, Hildy." Elizabeth headed out the door.

I didn't mind working on Friday nights. The "early to bed, early to rise" farming gene missed me completely, but I loved helping with the food that came from our kitchen.

I watched the smiling candle melt into a fiendish grin.

Little candle burning hot
Do we have a ghost or not?

Huge pots of Nan's chunky applesauce cooled on the stove; the aroma of cinnamon filled the kitchen. Nan's applesauce is famous in these parts, and bottling it fresh was a family enterprise.

My mother opened the box of new applesauce labels she and Elizabeth had created. It had a photo of Nan looking caring and rural.

GRANDMA NAN'S
Homemade Country Applesauce
Biddle Family Orchards
Banesville, New York
From Our Home to Your Table

Mom, the marketing brains of the family, said *grandma,*
homemade, and *country* were buzzwords to success. She
was cutting blue-checked fabric to put over the jar lids.
Mom's strawberry blond hair was pulled back in a braid,
the freckles on her cheeks at their peak as summer was
ending. People say I look a lot like her, which is such a
compliment.

"I heard the Hardines might be selling their place dirt
cheap," Nan said. The Hardines lived next door to the
Ludlow house.

"The Schmidts on Red Road are thinking about selling, too," Mom added. "And I don't know if the Hortons
can make it."

That was Lacey's family. "Not even with a good harvest this year?" I asked.

"We don't know what they had to borrow to get
through the last two years, Hildy."

"And they're not big enough to do a pick-your-own
business," Felix added. We had forty acres and counted
on school groups and the tourist trade to keep going. "If
we had to rely on just selling to wholesalers, the way the
grocery market's changed, we'd be on the street."

"I'd sell a kidney first," Nan muttered.

She always threatened to do that.

Nan checked the caramel sauce for her apple cake, then took two pans of apple brownies from the oven. The big wooden kitchen table was piled high with apple chutney, apple syrup, apple brown Betty, and apple bread. Juan-Carlos, our best worker, was packing the food into crates. I sipped a glass of Nan's cider. We Biddles have unfiltered cider flowing in our veins.

Mom looked up, her eyes sparkling. "Okay, everyone, what's the underlying reason that people buy apples?" As vice president of the county's Apple Alliance, she's always asking the big apple questions.

"Because they taste good," Elizabeth offered.

"Go deeper," Mom said.

"They're good for you," Elizabeth added. This was true—apples were low in carbs, had no fat, were a major source of fiber—a dieter's dream because they fill you up.

"Color," I mentioned. "Crunch, crispness."

Uncle Felix sat at the table, picked a Jonagold apple from a crate, and held it up. His face was tired from working all day, but his eyes shone when he held the fruit. There was something unusually tender in the way he said, "I think it's because of something we all remember and want to hold on to."

Mom smiled and wrote that down. Felix can be a philosopher, depending on his mood. He tried to sneak an apple brownie.

29

"I saw that, Daddy." Elizabeth snatched it from his hand. "You know what the doctor said."

The doctor said Felix needed to lose seventy pounds, and never had a man been less committed to the process.

"Man wasn't meant to be thin," he complained. "It's unhealthy."

Nan ladled applesauce into sterilized jars. "I'll tell you what's unhealthy—what's happening over on Farnsworth Road."

"Let's not start in with that," Felix grumbled.

Elizabeth beamed. "Hildy's writing about it."

All the adults turned to me.

"Just a little," I muttered. My family didn't think much of the Ludlow legend.

"She went to the courthouse today," Elizabeth added.

"It was during my study hall," I explained. This news wasn't going over big.

Thankfully, the phone rang. Being a teenager, I lunged for it. "Hello?"

"This is Sheriff Metcalf calling for Felix."

"Oh, hi, it's Hildy."

He didn't respond to that. I handed the phone to Felix. "It's the sheriff."

"Kind of late to be calling," Nan said.

It was ten-thirty. I tried to read Felix's face.

"Uh-huh . . . , " he said into the phone.

All females present listened.

"Where was he found?" Felix said flatly.

Where was who found?

"I see," Felix said, which told us nothing, but one look at his face said something big was up.

Finally, he hung up and sighed deep.

Nan wiped her hands on her apron, waiting.

Felix said, "The body of a man was found in the grove of apple trees on the Ludlow property a few hours ago. Doesn't look like he was from around here."

Elizabeth stood there frozen. "He's dead?"

Felix nodded. "The sheriff said they've secured the area. They've got some extra help coming from the state troopers."

"Was he murdered?" Elizabeth whispered.

"The sheriff's not saying, but he died somehow."

"That grove of apple trees is where old man Ludlow died," Elizabeth said nervously.

"Don't start with that bunk!" Felix snapped.

Her face got red.

The clock tick-tocked.

MacIntosh, my border collie, trotted up to me and stood guard.

I scratched his thick fur, looked up at the embroidered sign Nan had sewn that hung on our kitchen wall—little green apples spelling out the words BUY LOCAL.

"Did this have anything to do with the attempted break-in?" I asked.

Felix shook his head. "The sheriff didn't say."

Nan stood by the window, looking through the sheer

lace curtains at the black sky. "Why did he call?" she asked Felix.

"I expect he's trying to keep ahead of the rumor mill."

"I don't remember the last time we had something like this happen in Banesville," Nan said.

For the first time I could remember, Felix locked the back door.

Chapter 4

❖❖❖❖❖❖❖❖❖❖❖❖❖❖❖❖❖❖❖❖❖❖❖❖❖❖❖❖❖❖❖❖❖❖❖

Murder is a big word in a small town.

The Banesville Farmers Market was buzzing with the news.

People picked sweet corn from Bucky Luck's truck and talked about it.

They drank fresh-squeezed grape juice from The Grapes of Roth farm stand and wondered what it could all mean.

They stopped at Allie's Applehead Dolls and shook their heads at the darkness of it all.

They lined up at Minska's Polish Bake Stand and talked about the rumors that were flying.

Heard the body had vampire marks around the neck.

Heard the ghost killed him at the door and then dragged him to the apple grove.

All this talk of murder might not be good for business.

I picked bruised apples from the front bins of our stand and tried to keep the mood light.

Most people want zero emotional trauma when they come to a farmers market. They want fruit without anguish, serious cider, and all the joys of a perfect fall day.

Elizabeth was weighing apples, pouring cider, making change, and hardly saying a word. She gets quiet when she's scared.

As September days go, it was drop-dead gorgeous, not a cloud in the sky. I looked down the open lane of the Banesville Farmers Market, which took over the circle in the square every Saturday. It was thick with people and produce—peaches, plums, heirloom tomatoes, summer squash, green beans, peppers, and apples of every type and stripe—Braeburns (my dad's favorite), Crispins, Honeycrisps, Pink Ladys, Jonagolds, Galas. Our customers aren't looking for Red Delicious. They'd gag at the sight of one. They understand what fruit can be.

My family's farm stand was smack in the middle of the market, too—the best place to be, according to Felix: "We get 'em coming and going."

Lev Radner, my second former boyfriend, leaned across the fruit bins. Our families' stands have been next to each other for years. "There's a new sign at the Ludlow place," he told me. "'The darkness is encroaching.'"

Terrific.

Lev went back to schmoozing with customers in his stand. "My dear madame, into your hand I place an apple,

but do not be deceived—it is so much more than that."
Lev worked hard at being larger than life.

I worked straight through until one o'clock; I'd been
up since five.

"Permission to fall apart," I said to my mother.

"Permission granted."

I took off my red apron; Elizabeth touched my hand.
"Be careful," she said.

"I'm just taking my lunch break."

"We *all* need to be careful."

I walked past Herman's Upstate Wine kiosk and the
apple crepe cart and got in the long line at Minska's Polish
Bake Stand. Minska waved to me.

"You know the last time there was a murder in Banesville?" the woman in front of me said to her friend. "Five
years ago, when little Sallie Miner was killed."

The other woman tsk-tsked.

I wanted to say something about calling that a murder,
but I wasn't sure what.

Sallie Miner was hit by a car. Her death was an
accident.

"I heard the body had scratches all over it," someone
else said.

Minska raised her eyebrows at me. Not too much
makes her nervous. She grew up in Communist Poland
and saw fighting in the streets when she was a girl.

"Keep your head," Minska said, and put two sausage
rolls in a bag for me.

"I'm trying."

I walked to the little park in town square, sat down on a bench, and ate my sausage rolls.

Tanisha's little white poodle came running up and jumped in my lap.

"Hey, Pook, how are things in the adorable dog world?"

Pookie wiggled and licked my chin.

"What do you think is happening in town?" I asked her.

Pen Piedmont, the editor and publisher of *The Bee*, walked by with a group of people hanging on his every word.

"We're committed to keeping the people of Banesville informed," he told them. "We'll tell you what we know when we know it. I can promise you that."

My truth-detection meter hit zero when he said that. When Piedmont bought *The Bee* last year, he promised he was committed to Banesville's youth. Two months later, he cancelled the high school internship program.

Pookie went ballistic, yipping and snarling until Pen was out of sight.

The harvesters were still working when I got home. They'd spread across the middle grove, picking the Gala apples and the last of the Asian pears. Juan-Carlos was up on a ladder, picking with the lightest touch—reaching, twisting, quickly putting apples in his big shoulder sack.

MacIntosh was running around the trees on canine orchard patrol.

"Big storm coming," Juan-Carlos said. There still wasn't a cloud in the sky. He pointed west to the hill where the old Ludlow place stood.

"What do you mean, Juan-Carlos?"

He was quiet for a moment, like he was listening for something. "People are afraid," he said.

"If you hear anything, will you let me know?"

He smiled. "I listened for your father. I will listen for you."

I smiled back. *"Buenas noches."*

"Buenas noches a ti, my friend."

I walked through the rows of trees.

Four years ago my dad wrote an exposé for *The Valley News* on how certain farms weren't providing fair conditions for their seasonal workers. Not everyone was glad when that series came out. A few orchard owners had to pay steep fines, but it made Dad a kind of hero among the harvesters. When he died, so many workers' came to his funeral. They had candles flickering for Dad at the workers' quarters on our land.

The Valley News went out of business, though. Not enough advertising. They used to compete with *The Bee* before Pen Piedmont took over that paper.

I walked up the worn path through the Fuji trees. Apple perfume filled the air, the breeze blew gently, the leaves swayed. When I was little, I thought the trees were dancing. I used to dance around them, too, with my hands waving in the air.

I snapped an apple off a branch and headed to Nan's garden. Her roses were still hanging on; her crawling vines of pink trumpet flowers wound around the arbor. I sat on the bench my dad had made out of thick tree branches.

MacIntosh lay down at my feet. I rubbed his head and thought of a day when my dad and I were sitting on this very bench.

"You know how to peel an apple, Hildy?" Dad took out his Swiss Army knife and began to cut away the peel from a fat, juicy apple just picked from one of our trees. I was eight at the time and not too swift with knives.

"Once you start cutting, don't stop until the peel comes off." Dad was a speed peeler; in seconds the apple was bare. He handed it to me.

"It's how you do anything, really," I remembered Dad saying. "You've got to start and not stop until the job is done."

Mom gave me Dad's Swiss Army knife after he died. I took the knife out now, opened the blade, held the apple I just picked, and sliced the peel off fast in one piece.

The Bee hit the street Sunday morning:

MURDER IN BANESVILLE
LUDLOW HOUSE CLAIMS NEW VICTIM!

Someone or something is terrorizing Banesville. Early Friday evening, the body of an unidentified man was found in the grove of apple trees on the Ludlow property. Eyewitnesses said the man had deep scratch marks on his face and hands, prompting frightened neighbors to wonder about the safety of their street. No word has come as yet from the sheriff's department on the cause of death, but the man's body was found on the site haunted by the ghost of Clarence Ludlow. Two murders happened there thirty years ago—could a murderous ghost be taking revenge again? Recent investigation by this paper has pointed to increasing signs of ghostly activity at the Ludlow house. As resident groups demand answers, a new warning sign appeared at the Ludlow front door:

WHO'S NEXT?

Frightened neighbors say they regularly hear terrifying sobs at night rising in the darkness. Many have even seen ghosts walking the property.

> "Everything here has changed—
> especially since Sallie Miner was killed,"
> said one Farnsworth Road resident. "I'm
> living in a nightmare with no way out."

The article ended with, *Where is the ghost now? That's what people want to know.* The Bee *is offering a reward to anyone with information leading to the arrest of the murderer.*

I was helping Nan and Mom put out Canadian bacon and apple corn bread for Sunday breakfast.

Uncle Felix threw *The Bee* down.

"He's exaggerating things!" I said. "Where are the facts about the break-in? Who's going to believe a ghost is a murderer? How do they know it's a murder anyway?"

Mom picked up the paper from the floor and read the front page, stern faced.

Elizabeth scrambled eggs at the stove. "Jackie Jowrey told me her aunt was at a party and a hand appeared from nowhere and wrote *Don't Go to Farnsworth Road* right on the wall!"

Nan raised her eyebrows. "That story has been floating around in different forms for years, honey."

Elizabeth sprinkled fresh dill in the eggs. "I'm just repeating what I heard!"

"Just because you hear something doesn't mean it's right," Felix warned.

"Then how do you know what's true?" Elizabeth put the eggs on a platter.

"It's like looking at an apple," Felix explained. "It's not about color, it's about what it's got inside."

Nan scooped scrambled egg whites onto Felix's plate, no corn bread. She'd put him officially on the Last Chance Diet.

"They're not a natural color," Felix complained.

"It's not about color, it's about what it's got inside." Nan was his mother and could get away with this.

Felix bowed his head. "Lord, for *some* of what we are about to receive, let us be truly grateful."

Chapter 5

❖❖

Monday Morning *Core* staff meeting. Room 67B.

On the table—Tanisha's recent pictures of life in Banesville. She was doing a town retrospective. She really could capture moments.

Puppies playing in the window of Pet People while kids watched and laughed.

A girl with a candied apple stuck in her hair.

A guy with vampire teeth in front of the old Ludlow place.

Darrell stood before us. "We have a big opportunity to get people to finally pay attention to the paper. Hildy, I need your copy ASAP on the Ludlow house stuff, including all the details about the dead body."

"I don't have any details on that, Darrell."

"Well, *The Bee* does. Quote them."

I shook my head. "I don't believe what Piedmont is writing. I'm not writing anything I can't check."

"Call the sheriff, Hildy. Call somebody."

"It's not that easy."

"Hildy could interview the ghost," Lev suggested. "That would be great for circulation. We could do a series—*Hamlet*'s ghost, the Ghost of Christmas Past, Casper." He put his arm around me. "But I'm not sure Hildy believes in ghosts."

Maybe the ghosts of old boyfriends.

I shook Lev's arm off. "I'm not writing there's a ghost until I have the facts that prove it. Mr. Loring said, 'If it's not an editorial, don't draw conclusions.'"

Darrell sighed. We'd been writing together since third grade, when we began *The Grammar School Gazette*. Our first headline was questionable:

WIGGLESWORTH, CLASS RABBIT, DIES MYSTERIOUSLY

It wasn't all that mysterious—Wigglesworth was old and slept a lot—but Darrell said we weren't sure of the cause of death.

"A mystery," he said, "would make more people want to read it." I never felt comfortable with that.

Darrell turned to Tanisha, T.R., and Elizabeth. "What do the rest of you think?"

"I agree with Hildy. We only write what we can double check," said Tanisha.

"I don't think we should be writing about it at all!" Elizabeth protested.

"We can't drag our feet on this story," Darrell insisted. "We have to get out there and be part of the dialogue."

"Let's show *The Bee* they're not the only game in town!" That was T.R., sportswriter supreme.

"This isn't Room Sixty-seven, right?" A guy I'd never seen before was standing in the doorway, looking lost.

"This is Sixty-seven B," I told him. "Sixty-seven is upstairs, all the way at the end of the hall."

"That's illogical," he said.

I laughed. "Welcome to Banesville High."

The overhead light flickered.

The guy looked at it for a minute, then he dragged a chair over, stepped up, and hit the side. Nothing happened. He hit it again and the flickering stopped.

He stepped back down, put the chair away, and left.

"Who was that masked man?" Lev asked.

He had very nice eyes, actually.

The guy stuck his head back in the doorway. "Zack Coleman," he said. "I started at this school last week."

And with that he was gone.

"Attention, students . . ."

The principal's deep voice crackled through the intercom. "Due to our collapsed roof problem, Monday's drama classes will not meet in the auditorium, but in the cafeteria. If you are not part of the Monday drama group,

44

do not go to the cafeteria unless you are having lunch." There was a pause, a click, then Mrs. Kutash, the principal, was back. "The physics lab has been temporarily moved to the art room. That is all."

"I'm not sure I got that." The new guy, Zack, opened a locker three down from mine.

"I'm not sure anyone did," I said.

He was wearing a black T-shirt with faded jeans. He was a little taller than me and had light brown eyes with very expressive eyebrows.

Mrs. Kutash's voice came on again. "If you are part of the Drama Club, please meet in the cafeteria for practice. One moment . . ." The intercom crackled. "Look, if you are in any drama group whatsoever, just go to the cafeteria." She sighed. "I promise to get this right eventually."

Zack looked at the ceiling. "Can she see us, too?"

"Probably. Big Mother is watching you."

He laughed as the sounds of pounding feet came toward us. Two girls wearing caps that read *Are You Desperate?* headed toward the cafeteria. *Desperate People* was the name of the fall play. It spoke for us all.

On my locker someone had taped a creepy picture of the Ludlow house and written across it, *The End Is Near.*

"So you're new in Banesville, right?" I asked him.

Eyes on *The End Is Near.* "Yeah."

"We have this issue in town."

He shouldered his book bag. "I heard about the ghost."

He took out a pen, walked to *The End Is Near* sign, crossed out *Near*, and wrote *Under Investigation*.

I laughed. "That's better. I take it you don't believe in ghosts."

He smiled. "I believe in science. What about you?"

I told him I was writing an article for the paper about it; I was trying to *assess* the situation.

"In any assessment you have to collect the data and separate what you can quantify from what you can't."

I said I was doing *that*.

The bell rang. "The temporary physics lab in the art room is which way?" Zack asked.

"Down the hall to the left, past the elevator that doesn't work. Take a right at the stairs that have been roped off. It's next to the cafeteria."

"*What?*"

"Just follow the desperate people."

"Just because you cheated on me, Jason, doesn't mean I'm desperate. You think the world needs to revolve around you? You think that your unfaithfulness is going to stop my life somehow and make me forget who I am?" Joleene Jowrey, the lead in *Desperate People*, was working herself into a dramatic froth on the makeshift stage in the cafeteria.

Lev played Jason. It was perfect casting. "You can think what you want, Monique," Lev declared. "You can weave it like you always do to be the victim, or you can finally begin to look at yourself."

He said something similar to me when I accused him of cheating.

Art imitates life: okay as a concept—unfun when it's all too true.

Lev tipped his hat and botched his line: "Monique, someday I hope you'll . . . um . . ." He looked at Mrs. Terser, the drama coach.

"'Find the courage to be who you really are,'" she shouted.

Lev said that.

It was a lesson for us all.

I headed down the hall past homecoming posters reminding one and all about the big election coming up for Homecoming Queen. Normally I don't care much about that, but this year Lacey Horton was running, and Bonnie Sue Bomgartner, who had never gotten over giving up the Apple Blossom crown to Lacey, was desperate to win. The other candidates were Chelsea Meeks and Joleene Jowrey's twin sister, Jackie.

I saw Lacey racing down the hall.

"I'm voting for you," I told her.

Her eyes seemed red, like she'd been crying.

"Lacey, are you okay?"

She nodded, bit her lip, and rushed down the hall past a homecoming banner.

PLAN EARLY — DON'T MISS THE DANCE

Even if I'd started planning last summer, I wouldn't be going this year.

That was one thing in town I didn't have to wonder about.

"I was thinking about our subpar love lives." Tanisha leaned back in the comfy brown chair at Minska's Cafe.

I sipped my iced white chocolate. "I try not to think about it."

"But facing the truth, Hildy, is empowering." Empowerment was her theme this year. Tanisha speared a piece of poppyseed cake with lemon icing. "So, the truth is, we can rest easy because there are no interesting guys at our school."

Being a fact-based person, I checked the list of guys, stopping briefly at Aaron Dean, but no—Aaron had that tendency to unwrap candy slowly and loudly at the movies.

Tanisha raised her hands in the air. "There is *no one* left for us to go out with. We can focus on something else."

"Don't you think that's depressing?"

"Only if I focus on it."

I burrowed into the green love seat. Minska wanted her cafe to feel like home. She had couches and bookcases among the booths and the counter—the whole place was happily eclectic. A customer went to the bookcase and pulled out a dictionary.

Nathan Forrester, my first former boyfriend, was at a table in the back. Tanisha had warned me about going out with him *and* Lev. I'd warned her about going out with Clive Ramsey, ace basketball star, who did a slam dunk with her ego when he dropped her three days before the prom to go out with a much less interesting girl from Chesterton.

"You know where we got stuck?" Tanisha asked. "We were looking for faithful, loving, perfect relationships—males who were always glad to see us."

"So?"

"We already have that."

"What do you mean?" I demanded.

She smirked. "We've got dogs."

I slurped the last of my drink and took out the creative writing paper I'd gotten back—unfairly graded (a B minus) by Mrs. Terser, drama coach *and* English teacher. I showed Tanisha the paper, pointing to the margin note Mrs. Terser had written:

How did it feel to stand on the pier and look at the water?

"How did it feel?" Tanisha asked me.

"It felt peaceful. I said that in the first line."

Tanisha shook her head. "You need to say something like . . . 'The peaceful morning wrapped around me like a warm blanket.'"

"Please!"

"She'd love that."

"You're asking me to sell out."

"I'm asking you to be realistic. The woman wants metaphors, Hildy. She's going to retire in a few years. You're not going to change her." Tanisha could snag an A from any teacher.

Minska was at the register, laughing deep and full. Everything about Minska was like that. When she's sad—it goes deep; when she's happy—everyone in the room gets a piece of it. I interviewed her for *The Core* last year, and not just because she's one of our best advertisers. She's had the most amazing life. Minska was a teenager in Poland when the Communists took control of the TV and radio stations.

"All we could get," she said, "was their agenda day and night. They thought they were stronger because they had the media and the tanks. They didn't understand what some people will do to fight for the truth."

What some people did was turn their televisions toward the street in protest. Other people walked their dogs every night when their favorite radio show used to be on.

Minska headed toward us. She was wearing an orange blouse and her signature black pants that billowed when she walked. Her hair was short, her earrings were long.

"How's the news business?" she asked.

"Complicated," I said.

"Important things usually are." She held out a plate of tiny meatballs. We speared two. "Ground veal, bread crumbs, nutmeg, salt. It's all how you put it together." She carried the meatballs to each table. "We have special guests

50

today." She pointed to me and Tanisha. "Young women reporters. Treat them well."

Everyone smiled at us until the front door opened and Pen Piedmont walked in with two other men. People jumped up and asked him if there was anything new about the murder.

His eyes sparkled. "We're following every lead, folks. We're trying to get all your questions answered. Our number-one priority is to get to the truth and make sure the streets in Banesville are safe."

It sounded like he was running for mayor.

Tanisha whispered, "It's code blue, Hildy."

We'd developed a color-coded warning system.

Red meant "Danger."

Purple stood for "Proceed with caution."

Blue was "Don't trust this person."

Black meant "What's going on?"

Sometimes we'd just point to a color to get the idea across.

"So what have you got that's good today?" Piedmont asked Minska.

Minska looked at the red SOLIDARITY poster on the wall—the sign of the freedom movement in Poland.

She smiled. "Would you like food, Mr. Piedmont? Or an uprising?"

Chapter 6

✿✿

"*Core* staff, we have made excellent progress in getting you an adviser."

Mrs. Kutash, our principal, turned smiling to Mr. Grasso, the athletic director. The light from her office window illuminated his neck whistle. I looked at Darrell, whose face had gone pale. Just last night his father had confiscated his police radio, and he wasn't up for any more bad news.

"*Core* staff, I'm delighted to inform you that Mr. Mike Grasso has offered to assist you with the paper."

Tanisha, Elizabeth, Lev, and T.R. froze.

She gestured grandly and Mr. Grasso leaped forward. He clapped his hands like he expected us to run out there and win the big one.

"I know that Mr. Loring was a great help to you all, and I'm sure that his inspiration will carry us through this season."

It was going to be a *long* season.

"I'm . . . well . . . not exactly a writer. But I do have a cousin who's worked at a lot of newspapers. I'll see if he can help." He paused like that might not be a good idea. "He takes some getting used to . . ." Another clap. "Okay, team. I've seen you all out there. I know what you've got inside." He pointed to T.R., our sportswriter, and said, "Keep up that good game coverage. You're the man!"

T.R. smiled bleakly. He was working on a think piece called "Why Homecoming Matters When You Have a Losing Team."

Darrell stumbled forward. Editors don't leap. "Mr. Grasso, thanks for . . . jumping in." Darrell turned to us. "We're going to make a difference this year, everybody." He passed out a sheet. "But we need to watch the mistakes in our copy. I've found some real bloopers in our back-to-school edition."

He passed a sheet around. All newspapers publish corrections, but ours were, well . . .

Oops!

A story in our back-to-school issue concerning teenage drinking mistakenly referred to beer as "bear." We want to emphasize that popping a couple of bears (or beers) isn't recommended by this paper.

Mrs. Perth's slide presentation, "My Vacation in Slovenia," was not on Thursday last week, as reported, but Wednesday. We apologize to Mrs. Perth, who had donned full native garb for the event. *Those wishing to see this multiscreen event and Mrs. Perth's outfit should contact the school office.*

Our apologies to the Sadie family, whose ad last week commemorating the death of their dog, Rosco, referred to Rosco as a "Great Dame." Rosco was all man. The Core *mourns his passing.*

Mr. Grasso looked down, smiling.

Darrell continued, "And listen, everybody, Career Day is in two days and we want *The Core* to have maximum presence. We want to get the inside story. *Think* about your interview questions, please."

Mr. Grasso scooped up a book, *So, You Want to Be a Journalist?* He flipped through the pages and read, "Getting a great interview isn't as difficult as one might think. All that's required is a complete knowledge of your subject and a prepared list of both insightful and hard-hitting questions. Always avoid any questions that can be answered by yes and no answers." He turned to us. "Any questions?"

No.

The staff took a collective gulp and stumbled out of the office.

Darrell whispered, "You realize we could fold with the wrong adviser. That happened to a friend of mine in Cincinnati. They got the school nurse for their paper. I'm not kidding! Their paper shrank into a newsletter and then it became extinct!" His whole body sagged.

"You're turning into Chicken Little," I mentioned.

The stage crew of *Desperate People* struggled past us,

carrying a heavy backdrop of a starry sky, but they couldn't hold on.

It crashed to the ground.

Darrell turned to me. "You know what, Hildy? Sometimes the sky *is* falling!"

I was in the second-floor bathroom of my house—a room so big, we had a chair in it. The light blue paint was peeling off the walls; it had been for years. This whole house needed an overhaul, but we didn't have the money for that. I looked at myself in the scratched bathroom mirror. I had shoulder-length strawberry blond hair, a small nose, a few freckles, sincere brown eyes; I was five-seven and a half, just like my mom.

Just like my dad, I had a fierce desire to find the truth and help others find it, too. A fierce desire can get you a long way in this world, but sometimes I wondered if I had the right stuff to be a good journalist. My notes were always a mess. I had a hard time leaving my opinions out of what I was writing. Dad said you can't approach a story thinking you know how it's going to turn out; you've got to let it show you.

MacIntosh circled me; border collies are always trying to herd something. I was working out my theory that the sheriff couldn't have liked the article in *The Bee* since it was sensational and exaggerated, and that if he was looking for a local reporter who would be sensitive and careful and promise to quote him accurately, he need look no further.

The problem is, I'd called his office and left six messages. He hadn't called me back.

I'd been calling the number for D&B Security in Boston where Houston Bule had worked, too, but I kept getting their voice mail: "This is D&B. We're out. Leave a message."

I didn't leave one.

I jutted out my chin and said to the mirror, "Sheriff Metcalf, I'm writing an article about the Ludlow house and I'm wondering if we could talk about the dead guy—"

Maybe I should say *deceased*?

Maybe instead of standing at this mirror, I should just call him again.

This time I got him.

"Sheriff, I want to write an article about what's happening at the Ludlow house, and I don't want to exaggerate anything."

"That would be refreshing."

I took a big breath. "I need to ask you about the dead guy."

"The death is being investigated. The coroner's report won't be out for a couple of weeks." He said it like he'd been saying those lines all day long.

"Was the dead man Donny Lupo of D&B Security?"

"Good Lord, Hildy, where are you getting your information?"

"I was at the courthouse on Friday."

He didn't say anything.

"Sheriff, all I want to do is get the facts straight."

He was quiet for a moment. "Then get them straight. There were no marks on the body and no apparent struggle. Quote my office as giving you the information."

I wrote that down. "Thank you! Was the dead guy Donny Lupo?"

"The dead man has been identified as Donald Lupo, co-owner of D&B Security in Boston."

"Yes!" I shrieked, writing it all down. "I mean, thank you." I hung up before he took it all back.

In my room, typing. No fact escapes my grasp.

The body of Donald Lupo, co-owner of D&B Security in Boston, was found dead in the grove of apple trees on the Ludlow property early Friday evening. "There were no marks on the body and no apparent struggle," said the sheriff's office, squashing rumors that the man had been viciously attacked. Earlier that morning, Houston Bule, a part-time security employee of D&B Security, was arrested on the Ludlow property, trying to break into the abandoned house . . .

I cut in the rest of my article about the break-in. Read it, reread it, fixed the tense, ran a spell check.

I jumped up, did a little dance.

In mid-shimmy, I had a thought. Should that be *squashing rumors* or *quashing rumors?*

57

I checked my dictionary.

Quashing . . .

I fixed my copy, sent the article to Darrell, felt a major rush of accomplishment.

Getting the words right is right up there with dancing.

Chapter 7

A mob of students wound around Joseph P. Buzz, correctional officer (aka prison guard). He was holding forth on "the worst dregs of humanity behind bars, and you can thank God that's where they are and they're being watched."

"Have you ever been scared in your line of work?" I asked him.

"*Nah* . . ." His chest enlarged. Tanisha took a photo of that.

"Wow," I said. "I'd sure be afraid in a job like that. How do you handle it?"

He hesitated. "You learn to deal with it."

"How do you do that?"

"Gun helps," some kid said, and the others snickered.

"No," Buzz insisted. "That's not it." He pointed to his head. "It's up here. I can't spend time thinking about fear. I got a job to do." For just a second his face softened. "I tell myself those guys are more scared than me. I tell myself that every day."

I wrote that down. "Thank you, Mr. Buzz."

I walked to the next table over. Elizabeth was interviewing a professional dancer. "I've always wanted to know what happens to a dancer's feet. I mean, do you have foot problems?"

The dancer groaned and took off her shoes—her feet were covered with Band-Aids. "That's the part people don't see," she said. Tanisha swept in and took several photos up close and personal.

T.R. was asking a plumbing contractor what was the thing he liked most about his work.

He laughed. "It's when I hear the suck in the drain and I know I got the blockage."

Darrell muttered happily, "Now, that's an inside story!" He grabbed my arm and pointed to a man who had just sat down at the table in front of a hand-printed sign that read JOURNALIST. "Do you know who that is, Hildy?" We watched as Mr. Grasso walked over to the man and slapped him on the back.

"That's Baker Polton," Darrell explained. "He used to be managing editor of *The Albany Dispatch*. He's the cousin Mr. Grasso was talking about."

"The one who takes some getting used to?" Baker Polton looked like he'd slept in his clothes.

Darrell pushed me forward. "Get something really good."

"I didn't know he was coming."

"Nobody did."

I took a deep breath; walked over. Mr. Grasso said, "Baker Polton, meet Hildy Biddle. Hildy's our top writer."

I smiled. "Thanks. Mr. Polton, I'd love to know about your career in journalism."

"In what respect?"

"Well, I guess, how did you—"

"You *guess*? Or do you have a real question?"

Mr. Grasso grimaced.

"I have *several* real questions, sir."

"Shoot."

My mind raced to find some. "What's the toughest story you've ever worked on?"

"Sarasota, Florida. Brutal double murder. I was one of the first on the crime scene. Blood everywhere. Couldn't get it out of my mind. The killer got off."

"Why?"

"Why what?"

I bit my lip. "Why did the killer get off?"

"Because he was rich, famous, and had a fancy-talking lawyer who derailed the jury."

I wrote that down. "How did you get into journalism, Mr. Polton?"

He leaned forward. "Don't you want to know who the guy was? Don't you want any of the details?"

"Well . . ."

Mr. Grasso closed his eyes.

Baker Polton pointed his finger at me. "Let me tell you something. Whether you're on a school paper or a top city daily, you don't shortchange an interview. You ask all the follow-up questions you can. You never know what might come out."

I nodded, feeling like a moron.

"And keep good eye contact. That shows confidence. Nobody opens up to someone who gets easily thrown." He leaned back. "'So, Baker,'" he said. "'Who was this murderer? What were the charges? Where was the trial? When did this happen? Why did it happen? How did you write it? How did it affect the way you see your trade? What are you doing sitting at this stupid table?'" He scratched his day-old beard.

I'm not the idiot you think, mister!

I asked him the questions, got the facts on the murderer.

"Spelling," he said.

"What?"

"Jon Graves. How did you spell it?"

"J-O-H-N—"

"Wrong. J-O-N."

I felt my face flame red. I knew better. "Why are you sitting at this table?" I asked him.

Baker Polton rose slowly. "I'm standing up for truth."

✤✤✤

I was in the high school library, trying to get over the complete humiliation of having Baker Polton take me down a few notches. There are three kinds of people in the world: the ones who want to help you, the ones who ignore you, and the ones who love to see you squirm. Polton ruled in the last category.

I'd researched him online and discovered he was a semi–big shot in midsize dailies, meaning he'd had some important jobs at daily papers in cities like St. Louis, Albany, Stamford, Springfield, and Tampa.

I wished I'd seemed more professional when I interviewed him.

Deep humiliation always comes with a soundtrack—over and over I could hear him saying, *No one opens up to someone who gets easily thrown.*

In my pocket was Baker Polton's e-mail address. Mr. Grasso had given it to me. "Just so you know, Hildy," he'd told me, "Baker's staying at my house for a while until he gets . . . situated. You might want to contact him. He knows a lot."

Contacting Baker Polton seemed right up there with approaching a rabid dog.

A chair moved next to me. The new guy, Zack, sat down.

"I thought you handled that Polton guy well in there."

There was a witness to my shame! Couldn't the floor just open up and—

"You stayed with him," Zack insisted. "You got some interesting stories out of him."

"He spooned them into my mouth," I said.

"No one will know that when they read it, Hildy."

That was a decent thought. Zack had quite a strong profile, actually.

He smiled warmly.

I did, too.

Tanisha walked by and pointed to her black sweater. Black meant "What's going on?"

Oh, please. Absolutely nothing.

Zack opened a book and Lev came over to our table. "There's been a P.A. sighting at the Ludlow place," Lev whispered.

"P.A.?" I asked.

"Possible apparition," Lev explained. "Sallie Miner's ghost, I heard."

"They should burn that place down," said Ryan Gallagher from the table behind us.

"Or blow it up," another kid suggested.

"That's kind of extreme," Zack said quietly.

"Look, man," Lev snapped, "we've got a problem here."

"I know," Zack answered.

"What do you know about it?" Lev demanded.

Zack was quiet for a minute. "Well, reports like this tend to build on themselves. Someone sees something a little weird, and the first thing that comes to mind is eerie. Then the rumors start growing, and people get scared. Just like now."

"That house has been a problem for years!" Lev insisted. "We've got weird people hanging out there day and night."

"I heard."

Lev snarled, "Maybe you've also heard that people have died on that property."

"I've heard that, too. Unfortunately, people die lots of places."

Mr. Nordstrom, the librarian, rapped his shut-up-or-leave pencil.

Lev stood there sputtering.

Zack smiled and went back to reading his book.

Quiet strength goes a long way with me.

Midnight.

I get courage at midnight. I think it's because it's the end of things and the beginning of things.

Dear Mr. Polton,

Hildy Biddle here. I'm sure you're busy, but

Don't cower. I deleted that.

Mr. Polton—

I enjoyed meeting you at Career Day and

Don't lie. I hated every minute of it. DELETE.

> Hey, Baker—
> Your attitude is awesome and

Big DELETE.

> Mr. Polton—
> I learned a lot from you at Career Day.

Not bad.

> And because of that, I need to ask you a question. Would you consider helping us on our school paper? I'm not sure if you would even be interested or if you have the time. What I am sure about is this—I want to be the best journalist I can be and I could use your help.
>
> Thank you for considering this.
>
> Hildy Biddle

I didn't send it right away.

I circled the computer, reread the e-mail again and again.

I pressed SEND.

Sleep wouldn't come.

The hall light cast a thin strip across my bedroom floor. My rug had geometric patterns, but at night in a dark room, it seemed like a crazy maze that I was trying to get through. I could hear MacIntosh sleeping by the bed.

How do you get around that dark room, Hildy?

That was a big question I had to figure out after Dad

died. His death was so shocking, so sudden, it made me feel like anything bad could happen—the earth could explode, the ocean could evaporate, the stars could melt in the sky.

Mom found a therapist for me to see. Her name was Gwen. I didn't want to go at first because I don't talk about my troubles with just anybody. I'd sit in Gwen's soft navy blue swivel chair and face the wall. It was easier to talk to a wall in the beginning.

"How are you feeling today, Hildy?"

"Awful."

"Are you feeling scared today?"

I was scared a lot that eighth-grade year.

"Can you describe the fear, Hildy?"

"No."

"Because sometimes when I'm scared," Gwen said in her soothing voice, "I feel a little like I'm in a dark room with all the lights out. Have you ever felt like that?"

I turned halfway toward her and nodded.

"And what do you do?" she asked.

"I guess I try to find the wall."

"That's right."

"I try to find the things I know are there and get to the bed."

"You look for things that are familiar," Gwen said. "And you know, that's what you've got to do now."

It took a while to find the real touch points of my life

again. But when I started looking, I realized they were everywhere—the orchard, my school, my friends, my family,
my dog.

I got out of bed, touched MacIntosh's head.
"Good dog."

I turned on the bed lamp and walked to my desk.

My laptop beckoned.

I checked my e-mail; spam, actually.

Thin thighs in thirty minutes

Delete.

If I don't get one thousand dollars by Thursday, I
will die. Can you help me?

Delete.

Are you naughty?

Nope. But you are. Delete.

Your request

I was about to zap it, then I saw the sender.

Baker Polton! He'd responded already.

I took a deep breath. This could be my big break. I
clicked on the message excitedly, up it popped:

Can't do it. I'm swamped.

B. Polton

I sat there looking at the screen.

Chapter 8

❖❖❖❖❖❖❖❖❖❖❖❖❖❖❖❖❖❖❖❖❖❖❖❖❖❖❖❖❖❖❖❖❖❖❖❖❖❖

On Friday morning *The Core* was published. My Ludlow house story was front and center, too. No typos, either, but there was some unfortunate wording in a classified ad:

DOG FOR SALE—Eats anything and is particularly fond of children.

I got ready for the onslaught of kids congratulating me on getting the facts right in my article.

That didn't exactly happen.

I walked through the hallways holding the paper as a visual aid, hoping someone would comment on it.

That didn't happen, either.

In biology lab, *The Core* was used to wrap up dissected frog carcasses.

Jerry Sizer used his *Core* to wipe mud off his boots.

It's best for journalists not to focus on the alternative uses for their work.

Didn't anyone care about the truth?

I walked to my locker, saw Zack rush by. "Great article!" he shouted on his way to class.

Finally! Too bad he couldn't stop and go into more detail.

I headed to the Student Center, where Joleene Jowrey was arguing with her twin sister, Jackie, about whether vampire marks were on the dead body. I walked up to them, doing my part as a truth teller.

"The sheriff told me there were no scratches on the body, no vampire marks, nada. Come on!"

"You come on, Hildy! You think the sheriff is going to tell the truth about that?" And they went back to arguing about whether the ghost was still on the property or roaming the streets looking for his next victim.

I walked past the DO NOT ENTER sign plastered across the auditorium door. I wondered when that collapsed auditorium roof would be fixed. It was one of many places in town that needed repair. I'd called the mayor's office and the Board of Ed about it, but hadn't gotten anywhere.

"Stay with a story," Dad always told me. "Stay with it until it makes sense."

"It's a fine day in Banesville, people," Mayor Frank T. Fudd boomed at the farmers market. "My, haven't we been given a sweet town?"

"Getting kinda sour around the edges," Felix muttered.

The mayor was making his presence known, walking

70

briskly down the open lanes, showing everyone within ear-shot that he wasn't worried about an ever-loving thing.

The pears and quinces were showing up at the market now. The aroma of apple cider filled the air. I was explaining to a customer that apples need to be refrigerated to keep their flavor. If you leave them out on the counter, no matter how pretty they look, they're going to get mealy in nothing flat.

The mayor strolled past our stand; I heard a woman reporter ask him, "What's the plan you're going to unveil to revitalize Banesville?"

I hadn't heard of any plan.

Mayor Fudd said, "Well, my office is always working on something new. That's what this administration is all about."

The reporter smiled brightly. She was wearing a Windbreaker embroidered with the words *Catch the buzz in Banesville . . . read* THE BEE. "Mr. Mayor," she continued, "I hear this plan is big."

"It's a humdinger all right," he acknowledged, chuckling.

I grabbed a notepad from my backpack and wrote that down. I told Mom I'd be right back and headed toward the mayor, who was saying, "We're looking ahead to tomorrow. We're looking at all the places where we can make things better for people and plot a strong course for our future."

He looked at me and smiled because, I guess, I represented the future. I smiled right back. "Mr. Mayor, I'm from the high school. I was wondering when our roof problem is going to be fixed."

His face got a little pink. "We're going to be taking care of all that."

"Do you have a completion date?" I continued.

He coughed.

"Have you thought about the danger of having a collapsed roof covered by a tarp on school property?"

He harrumphed. "I take the safety of every citizen of Banesville seriously."

"How's the Lupo investigation coming?" I asked.

"Sheriff Metcalf is on that, covering every lead."

"Any word on the cause of death?"

He glared at me. "The sheriff will be issuing a statement."

The woman reporter wasn't too happy I'd barged in. She shouted, "Your revitalization plan, Mr. Mayor. What is that about?"

He smiled. "Making Banesville a better place."

I asked, "Does the revitalization plan involve the high school, Mr. Mayor?"

Irritation flashed across his face; he walked away from me. "You ask a lot of questions, young lady."

How else do you find things out?

I've been asking questions all my life. My first official word as a baby wasn't *Mama* or *Dada*. It was *Whazzat?*

All day long I'd point at things.

Whazzat?

72

"Newspaper," Dad would answer. "Dirt . . . doggy . . . doo-doo . . . *Don't touch that, Hildy!*"

Why is the sky blue?

Why do birds fly?

Why does Mrs. Johnson's breath always smell funny? Mrs. Johnson was my kindergarten teacher.

Why does Mrs. Johnson's voice get like that?

I kept asking until someone looked into it. Turned out Mrs. Johnson had gin in her water bottle. By the time we got to phonics, she was feeling no pain.

She got a leave of absence and we got a new teacher.

Who says kids don't have power?

A woman in a purple cape was at Allie's craft stand, holding up an Applehead Doll—the apple heads wrinkled up when they dried, making this a popular gift for people over thirty. She was saying to Allie, "I have seen this craft in my homeland, Romania. A wise woman made them—most respected."

Allie liked that.

That woman in the cape walked down the lanes of the market like a queen, pausing briefly to look at things.

I followed her and she stopped at our stand, smiling warmly at the BIDDLE FAMILY ORCHARDS sign, picked up a jar of Nan's chunky applesauce, and held it to the light like she knew something deep about it.

"How much, dear one?" she asked Elizabeth in a smoky, accented voice.

"Six dollars."

"Where have you been?" Nan asked me.

"Investigating," I said.

The caped woman looked at me; her dark eyes bored through me. She took out a beaded coin purse and slowly unfolded the bills. She handed them to Elizabeth and smiled broadly.

Then she moved on.

"Who *is* that woman?" Elizabeth asked me, putting the money in her apron.

"Another weird tourist?"

On Sunday *The Bee* broke the news.

RENOWNED PSYCHIC MADAME ZOBEK TO SETTLE IN BANESVILLE

She was so renowned, *The Bee* proclaimed, that she was considering an offer to appear regularly on the new hit cable show *Hair-Raising Haunts*.

People came to her from all over the world to seek her wisdom. She had come to town because of the Ludlow place. "It drew me," she explained in the article. "I felt the spirits of the dead calling me to come. I cannot tell how long they will ask me to linger, but I must obey."

"Hopefully, not too long," Minska said when she read the article.

Tanisha and I were sitting in a window booth at Minska's. I dipped a deep-fried apple slice into thick caramel sauce, watched the caramel drip slowly onto the plate. Caramel takes its sweet time. It's my favorite flavor.

Tanisha took out her latest photos of life in Banesville. "It's getting harder for me to photograph people who don't seem a little nervous, Hildy. I see it on their faces."

I looked at the photographs of stern-faced growers in the Red Road orchards, of mothers rushing into cars with their children.

"You see this one?" She held up a shot of Main Street on a Saturday night with not a car in sight. "Since the dead guy was found, people aren't going out the way they used to."

It was dinner time and Minska's wasn't packed with people, either—that hardly ever happened.

I looked at the photos of Minska's father on the back wall. He worked in the shipyards in Gdansk, Poland. That's where the protests began that ultimately led to Poland's freedom. Minska's father was jailed and beat up, but he never stopped believing that Poland would be free. "The stirring for freedom was everywhere," Minska told me in our interview last spring. It was the best article I've written. People asked for copies of it long after it ran.

The man in the booth behind us groaned. He'd been groaning for a while now. All I could see was his back. Minska went over to him. She was wearing her billowing black pants, a white shirt, and silver hoop earrings. "Do you need a taxi, sir?"

"You got taxis in the happy apple valley?" he said, slurring his words.

"We've got one," Minska responded.

He moaned again.

"Do you need a doctor?" she asked.

He waved an arm. "Not sick."

Minska walked away, but kept her eye on the man as she dusted the photo of the woman who was a leader in the early workers' strikes in Poland.

"She was a factory worker," Minska had said to me. "So brave; always ready to expose wrongdoings. Her name was Anna. She was my hero. During the strikes she said, 'I knew that I could not conquer great wrongs myself, so I started with small things.'"

I ate my apple slice slowly.

Now we heard ripping noises in the booth.

Tanisha turned around and asked the man if she could help.

"Not at the moment," he snarled.

She turned back. "It's code purple, Hildy."

Purple stood for "Proceed with caution."

I stood and looked. The man was ripping a newspaper up into little shreds. He grunted, "This is the only cure for bad writing." He tore an article in half.

I sat back, shocked.

It was Baker Polton!

He sure looked disheveled. "Are you all right?" I asked him.

"Depends on your definition of *all right*." He ripped up more of the newspaper, *The Albany Register.* "This used to be a great newspaper. I used to work at this paper. You know what it is now?" Tanisha picked up a shred. "Puff and puke." He sat back like he had a headache. "You want to know why I walked out on this job? I was managing editor. They told me I couldn't write a story that questioned the lousy emissions ratings for a certain kind of SUV that just happened to be sold by one of our biggest advertisers. I told them to stick it." He looked at me. His eyes seemed a bit cloudy. "Why do you want to be a reporter?"

I thought for a second. "I care about the news and getting it right."

"Do something else. The field's changing too much. Don't get sucked in."

"But—"

"They're going to ask you to believe that entertainment is news. What are you going to tell them? They're going to put things that don't matter on the front page and the ones that do on page twenty. They're going to tell you that flash and sex sell papers and that's all people are looking for these days. They're going to reduce your copy to sound bites and slogans and if they can figure out how to make a scratch-and-sniff midsized daily, believe me, they'll do it."

"My dad was a reporter, Mr. Polton."

"Mine, too." He looked out the window. "*Chicago Tribune.* City Desk. He knew Royko." I decided not to mention our fly. Baker Polton sat straighter. "Where's your dad working?"

"He died."

He glanced at me. He had flecks of gray in his thinning hair; he had a thick neck, too. He went back to examining his beer bottle. "What are you working on?"

I told him about the Ludlow place, how the fear in town was growing. "I'm not sure how to write about fear."

"Don't write about fear. Write about people who are afraid." He finished his beer.

"That's really good advice, sir."

He pointed a finger at me. "And remember what Pete Hamill says—during the first twenty-four hours of any big breaking story, about half the facts are wrong."

I didn't know that. "How do you figure out what's true?"

"Keep questioning people. Confirm everything."

"You know a lot," I said.

He looked sad. "About some things." He signaled Minska behind the counter. "Could you call me that cab?"

"I already did." Al's Apple Taxi pulled up in front of the restaurant.

Tanisha and I walked him out to the cab.

"Where's home, pal?" the driver asked.

"Home . . ." Baker Polton said it like it didn't exist. "I'm at my cousin's place. Renshaw Road."

***

Home.

In my room. Laptop ready.

I sent the e-mail, short and sweet.

Mr. Polton,

How do you stand up for truth?

Chapter 9

✿✿✿

Baker Polton stood rumpled at the front of Room 67B and looked at the VERITAS sign that was still hanging crooked on the wall. He was wearing gray pants and a stained blue shirt. Mr. Grasso stood in the doorway. There was hardly room for all of us.

I walked up. "Mr. Polton, thank you for coming."

"Somebody had to rescue you from Grasso."

Mr. Grasso cracked his knuckles and grinned.

"And by the way," he added, "I appreciate persistence."

I smiled and found a seat.

Mrs. Kutash gushed that, as our principal, she was delighted to announce that Mr. Polton had agreed to be our adviser for the rest of the semester, and did we realize how fortunate we were to have a journalist of his standing to help us with the paper?

"Adults who selflessly volunteer their time to further

the cause of education give a great gift to the school and future generations."

"We'll see," Polton said.

Mr. Grasso cleared his throat in a kind of warning.

Mrs. Kutash smiled nervously.

Baker Polton sneered at the whiteboard in the corner that listed some upcoming stories for our next edition:

Great date movies
Joys of the harvest
Ongoing roof repair
New football uniforms

Someone had written *All Ghost, All the Time*. Lev, probably.

Then Baker Polton shook out the last issue of *The Core*; pages fell on the table. "What are you working on that people will care about next week?"

Darrell, Tanisha, T.R., Elizabeth, Lev, and I looked at each other.

No one wanted to go first.

He turned to the whiteboard and wrote: NOBODY WANTS OLD NEWS. He underlined it.

"This is a newspaper, kiddies. A newspaper needs stories. What have you got?"

Darrell mumbled that we were following the Ludlow house story and the murder.

"Alleged murder," Baker corrected. "What have you got that's new on Lupo?"

Darrell looked desperately at me.

"I got some good quotes from the sheriff," I explained.

Hands on hips. "What have the rest of you got?"

Lev half raised his hand. "We're doing in-depth interviews with our best advertisers."

"Why?"

"We thought they'd give us more money if we did."

Baker Polton tapped his marker on the whiteboard and wrote DON'T SUCK UP. "It'll always come back to bite you in the butt." Mrs. Kutash's face reddened.

T.R. said, "I'm thinking about doing something about the dangers of football injuries—concussions, things like that."

"Now, that's a feature." Baker Polton wrote it on the whiteboard. He put a slash through *New football uniforms*.

"What's news?" he asked us.

We looked at each other.

"*What's news?*" he asked again. He held up a copy of Sunday's *Bee*. "It's not this."

BANESVILLE BRACES FOR MORE ATTACKS

"Well?" Baker Polton demanded.

We turned to Darrell because editors are supposed to know these things. He stammered, "Well, it's, uh . . . it's kind of, in actuality . . . reporting what's going on."

Baker Polton half nodded. "So that means a newspaper can report anything that's going on."

Darrell shook his head. "No, not exactly. I mean, it could, but that's not the point."

Baker Polton stared at him. "What's the point?"

I gulped and added, "The point is it has to matter."

"To whom?"

"To the readers," T.R. offered.

"And who decides what matters?"

There was a long silence, except for coffee sipping.

"We do," I said.

"And it's hard," Darrell added.

Baker Polton squashed his Styrofoam cup. "If it ever gets easy, do something else."

It didn't get easier.

"He's kind of angry," Elizabeth whispered to me.

"I'd say he's really angry, Elizabeth."

"How come we got him for an adviser?"

I decided not to confess.

"He scares me, Hildy. I don't think he's going to like my writing."

That was probably true—Elizabeth's strength was in visual design, not sentence structure.

"I don't think he likes much of anything," Tanisha said.

We were getting ready to have our egos decimated by Baker Polton. He had asked each of us to give him what we thought was our best recent piece of published writing, and now we were going to discuss it. He took a seat at the table. We shoved our seats around him.

"There's more room in an elevator," he said gruffly. "Let's hit the ground running. *Elizabeth Biddle*."

She raised a timid hand. "Present."

Baker Polton put his feet on the table, leaned back in his chair, and read, "'The long, lonely high school corridors seemed to be filled with the whispers of the graduating seniors who had left their marks on us all.'"

Elizabeth smiled nervously.

He looked up. "Did the seniors draw on you with laundry markers?"

"Why, *no . . .*"

He slashed through her copy, wrote in red, *We won't forget the graduating seniors.* "Keep it simple, kid. This is journalism, not creative writing."

Elizabeth's face fell.

He read a few more lines about "'their dreams for the future wafting up like clouds floating in the deep blue sky.'"

Elizabeth squirmed.

He pushed back his reading glasses and looked around the table. "Less is more. Less description, more facts. Only describe if it means something. The killer had one arm. The mayor was seven feet tall. The hero was deaf. For now, let's not care if the sky was blue. If it's plaid, mention it."

He put a piggy bank on the table. "From now on, each unnecessary word costs you one dime." That could wipe us out, particularly Elizabeth. Baker Polton picked up my article on the Ludlow house. "*Hildy* Biddle . . . is this paper a family-run operation?"

"We're cousins," Elizabeth explained.

I held my breath.

He waved his glasses. "Good, tight opening, nice quotes from the sheriff, but here's where you lose me." Glasses back on. "'Many neighbors wonder about the safety of a house that seems to hold so many mysteries.' What does that mean?"

"I was just trying to show that—"

"You lost the color."

"I don't understand."

"Did you interview the people?"

I nodded.

"What did they say?"

"I was just trying to get everything in and—" I lowered my head. Did I really just say that?

"But you had space for this: 'The mayor's office said that the town was looking into the situation.' Does that refer to the house or the murder?"

"That's what they said when I called."

"Did you ask to speak with the mayor?"

"Not for this article. I did talk to him at the market on Saturday."

"But in this piece you didn't. Polton's First Law— Always ask three follow-up questions."

He made it sound so easy.

"Could you give us an example?" I asked.

He ticked them off. "Who's looking into the situation? What's being done in case of an emergency? When will the mayor be taking questions from the press?"

I wrote those down. "Thanks."

"You might not get an answer, but they'll know they can't ignore you."

I asked, "Mr. Polton, how do we get people to take us seriously?"

"Start by taking yourselves seriously."

I checked with the sheriff to see if the coroner's report was out yet. It wasn't.

I called D&B Security to see if anyone wanted to spill their guts about Houston Bule and Donny Lupo. I got the answering machine again.

I went home, dragging my seriousness with me.

It wasn't easy there, either.

Hildy, did you take the supplies to the field?

Hildy, the school tour is here.

Hildy, please stop wasting time and get down here now.

I'm not wasting time—I'm writing!

I closed my laptop and headed down the long stairs past the old grandfather clock. My great-grandmother had painted apple blossoms on the wood.

How many generations of Biddles had walked down these stairs?

Sweated over the harvest?

Prayed for good weather?

Kept going no matter what came at them?

I walked into the kitchen. The big blue work calendar was on the yellow wall. Being fall, there was so much going on.

HILDY—
Wednesdays (3–5), School Tours.
Fridays (5–8), Work at Farm Stand.
Saturdays (5–3), Farmers Market.

Elizabeth's schedule was just as crazy, except for Wednesdays. She was too sweet to keep little kids in line— she helped Nan with the baking for the market instead.

Uncle Felix was reading *The Bee*. "Who's writing this stuff?" he asked, throwing it down.

This paper sure got thrown down a lot.

I picked it up. "If people don't work hard to get the truth and print it, this is the best we'll get," I told him. "If people just get mad at the paper and don't demand better reporting, nothing will change. I'm trying to change things."

He looked at me. "You sound like Mitch."

I smiled. Mitch was my dad.

Felix sighed. "He was the fighter, I was the farmer."

"You fight the weather," I reminded him.

"Mitch was always marching off to right some wrong." Felix looked miserably at his bag of rice cakes. "Might as well gnaw on cardboard."

"No calories in cardboard," I told him.

He got up grumbling and headed outside.

I sat down and opened *The Bee* to Madame Zobek's new column.

"It is the beginning of a great gathering," she wrote. "I sense there is a deep moving here. I sense a great darkness."

She wrote that she had personally spoken to several spirits at the Ludlow place and they told her there were many more who would be joining them.

Terrific . . .

I didn't like the way Madame Zobek was making her presence known. She was open for business in a small store next to the offices of *The Bee*. I'd walked by it the other day. She'd hung thick purple curtains over the window, hung a black and silver sign on the door: RING THE PSYCHIC DOORBELL.

Tanisha got a photo of the sign.

"If she's really psychic," Zack said when he saw Tanisha's photo at school, "why does she need a doorbell?"

But people of all ages began to ring the bell and seek her advice. She had a brochure, too.

Advice from the ages on . . .

love

life

family

career direction

medical problems
depression
addictions
college choices
the stock market
pet compatibility selection
how to chose a contractor for
a home remodeling project

The list went on and on.

Cash only.

Chapter 10

Joleene Jowrey stood on the makeshift stage in the cafeteria, faced Lev Radner's smirking face, and delivered one of the worst lines ever written in the history of the stage.

"Just because you don't love me anymore, Jason, doesn't mean I don't still love you. I will love you until the rivers run dry and the stars fall from the sky."

I swear, this play made you desperate.

"I need you to give me more with that line, Joleene," Mrs. Terser shouted. "Make me a believer."

Joleene looked at Lev, who belched. She took his hand and said, "*Just* because you don't love me anymore, Jason, doesn't mean I don't still love you. I will love you until the stars run dry and the rivers fall from the—*wait*—" They both started laughing.

"Let's get our metaphors straight," Mrs. Terser directed. "Rivers run dry, stars fall . . ."

I put on my *Are you desperate?* cap and headed off to a very long day.

Lessons came at me fast and furious.

In history I learned that fiefdoms stink.

In English I learned that *Moby-Dick* wasn't just about sea life.

In chemistry I learned it's a really bad idea to add water to sulfuric acid.

In room 67B, *The Core*'s office, I learned how to get to the heart of a story.

Baker Polton had commandeered the desk in room 67B. He had put a photo of a pretty, smiling woman with a little boy on it, too.

"Nice picture," I said.

He nodded as Royko buzzed near the food heap. "How do you kids work in here?"

I shrugged, looked back at his photo. "Is that your family?"

"My ex-wife and son."

"Sorry."

He gazed long and hard at that picture. "Not as sorry as I am." Then he leaned forward in his chair and said, "Biddle, are you hungry enough to get to the heart of the Ludlow story?"

I felt my face get hot. "I'm plenty hungry!"

"Then explain to me why you haven't contacted any-one who knew Sallie Miner."

"I've been doing other things," I stammered. "I've

been calling D&B Security. I just get the answering machine."

"That's not what hungry looks like. Let me see your notes."

This wasn't going to be pretty. I took my notes out of my book bag, lay them folded and crumpled at his desk.

"Wait, there's more."

I grabbed some from the side pocket, pushed my note-pad toward him, took a piece of paper from my pocket. I tried to smooth it.

He picked up a wrinkled sheet. "Polton's Second Law—If you're not organized, it'll kill you." He spread out the sheets. "Why aren't they numbered?"

"I never thought of that."

He looked at one page from my notebook when I went to the courthouse. He underlined two words and handed it back to me.

Boston

Martin

"Don't you think it's odd," Baker said, "that with all the security companies here in New York, D&B Security from Boston was checking out the Ludlow property?"

"What do you think it means?"

"I don't know. But it's a hole in the story. Make a list of what you don't know and where you might find it."

"I don't know anything about Sallie Miner except that she went to Banesville Elementary."

I grabbed the phone, called the school, asked if anyone remembered who Sallie's third-grade teacher was.

"Oh, yes," said the secretary. "That would be Eileen Leary. She's living in Madison, Wisconsin, now."

I turned to Baker excitedly. "I got a lead on the teacher."

"Follow it."

I called directory assistance, got her phone number.

Hildy Biddle, ace reporter, had been let loose.

I made the call. A woman answered. I said, "I'm trying to reach Eileen Leary—who taught third grade in Banesville."

"That's me . . . ," she said cautiously.

"Mrs. Leary, I'm Hildy Biddle. I'm researching an article about the Ludlow house in Banesville for my high school paper. I'm trying to determine facts from fiction. Can I ask what you remember about Sallie Miner?"

"Well, she was always scared of that house, living as close to it as she did."

I was writing. "Really? What was she afraid of?"

"The ghost. Some unnamed evil. Sallie had such an imagination. She was always telling us about seeing something unusual. I think it became her reality. She was a good student. She always brought a valentine for every child in the class, very thoughtful. Have you talked to her father?"

"No." I couldn't imagine doing that.

"He and his wife divorced after the accident. He's living in Miami, I believe. He was a good man. I remember him coming to Parents' Night. I think his first name is Larry. Larry Miner. I don't know if he would talk to you, but it's worth a try."

"Thank you, Mrs. Leary. I'm trying to find the truth."

She sighed. "That would be most welcome after all this time. Good luck to you."

I sat back in my chair, numbered my notes, and showed them to Baker.

"You know, Biddle, whoever breaks this story open can really help this town."

"I want to do that!" I hit the Miami phone book online.

There were eleven Lawrence Miners in the Miami area. But what would I say when I called?

Hi, is this the Lawrence Miner whose little daughter, Sallie, was killed five years ago?

I couldn't do that, could I?

"The thing is," I said to Mom, "Baker says that breaking the Ludlow story open could really help Banesville, so I've got this mission now to track down every lead, and I've hardly got time for homework, much less doing school tours at the orchard."

"I know you'll find a way to fit it all in," Mom answered with a supreme lack of compassion as the yellow

94

school bus pulled up the driveway. "Here come our little guests."

Twenty-nine first-graders, to be exact. They ran off the bus screaming. It was school visiting day at the orchard.

"Remember, Hildy," Mom said. "We want them to care about where their fruit comes from."

"Cantwell!" I screamed at the six-year-old boy who swiped a pile of Nan's chunky apple brownies after major warnings from me *not* to eat, suck, destroy, bruise, toss, spit upon, or touch them in any way. "If you eat them, Cantwell, if you move or do anything other than breathe, your time in the orchard barn will be over. Got it?"

Cantwell nodded, which technically was moving, but I decided to let it go. I looked at the other children, who looked back at me to see if I meant it and decided I did. The teacher and the parent helpers were off in the corner by the Johnny Appleseed poster.

The orchard barn was where we gave demonstrations, where we had our small market.

I took out my guitar and taught them a song that only required three chords—C, D, and E minor—the only ones I knew how to play.

Up, down, all around,
Apples begin from a seed in the ground.

Juan-Carlos showed them the hand motions. He really got into this.

"Arriba! Arriba!" he shouted, which means "Up! Up!" in Spanish.

We sang the song over and over. Then I read them the story of Johnny Appleseed's love of apples, his total focus on one fruit, how his commitment to a dream benefited generations to come. I glared at Cantwell. *"Now,* everybody, it's time for your snack!"

The kids descended on the plate of apple brownies like moths to a light source. A little girl, Sara, ran up and hugged me. "You have a pretty face, Hildy."

I hugged her back. "You have a pretty face, too."

Missy Grimes marched up, a very complicated little girl. I used to babysit for her. She had a bandage on her elbow. "Hug me, Hildy! Hug me, too!" I gave her a big one.

Missy's eyes were wide. "I saw something and it was big! Huge, even!"

"Really?"

I babysat Missy last summer and was exhausted by the experience. Missy claimed to see lots of big things—giant bats, enlarged worms, gargantuan bees—all swooping down to get her. Her parents were going through a nasty divorce. Mrs. Grimes kept calling me to babysit again, too. I'd been avoiding her.

Missy grabbed both my hands. "I *saw it,"* she insisted. Then she lowered her voice. "I can't tell the other part. But you can read about it!"

"What do you mean?"

"What do we say, children?" the teacher asked, be-

96

ginning to steer the kids onto the bus with their apple bags.

"Thank you!" shrieked the first-graders of Banesville Elementary.

I took Missy's hand. "Missy, what are you talking about?"

"It's a secret," she whispered, and ran onto the bus. She sat at the window staring out. She always seemed lonely.

The bus pulled away.

You can read about it.

I didn't like the sound of that.

Chapter 11

✤✤✤✤✤✤✤✤✤✤✤✤✤✤✤✤✤✤✤✤✤✤✤✤✤✤✤✤✤✤✤✤✤✤✤✤✤

"I hear up by Ludlow's place there's more coming," Crescent Furl, owner of the A to Z Convenience Store, said to me. She had the headache medicines up front at the counter now—they used to be in the back.

I grabbed a bottle of water from her refrigerator. "What do you mean?" I asked.

Crescent sniffed. "All I heard is some talk."

To get Crescent to really talk, you had to buy more. I grabbed two Hershey bars, peanuts, a pocket Kleenex, and put five dollars on the counter. "Tell me."

Crescent rang up the order slowly. "It's not like I'm some kinda telegraph center."

I smiled. "Crescent, you know everything going on in town."

She liked that. "I hear," she said, "they saw another one."

"Another what?"

"Another ghost," she said ominously.

"Who saw it?"

"Didn't hear who, just what."

A tired mother with four children came in. The kids were screaming, running everywhere. More people came in. The store was close to packed. Not the time to try to talk to Crescent.

I didn't have to wonder long.

The Bee hit the street with a special edition blaring the news.

ANOTHER LOCAL GIRL INJURED BY LUDLOW'S GHOST

CROWDS SURGE ONTO FARNSWORTH ROAD

The name of the girl was being withheld "to protect the innocent," but the girl went into vast detail about biking down Farnsworth Road and all that she saw in the upstairs room of the Ludlow house.

"It was big," she asserted. "Huge, even."

Specifically, it was a floating head, and after she saw it, a branch fell from a tree in the Ludlow yard and scared her, causing her to fall off her bike. She was taken to the emergency room and kept under observation into the evening. There was a spooky picture of the Ludlow house with a new sign front and center.

Guess What's Next?

There was a picture of Sallie Miner, too, under the heading "Are Our Children Safe?"

What power was causing branches to fly off trees and attack children? That was another question *The Bee* pursued exhaustively, with help from Madame Zobek.

"There is some property so haunted that even the trees are taken over," she wrote. "I am concerned about the safety of Banesville's children."

What about teenagers? Are we safe?

And what about good old Reality?

No one would take Missy Grimes seriously.

Right?

And it's not like *I saw something and it was big, huge, even* is all that distinctive.

But I couldn't seem to let it be.

I could go talk to her, I suppose. I could ask her mother. I could mind my own business.

No, reporters can never do that.

I talked to Baker, who said, "Well, you could always babysit."

That seemed awfully extreme.

In case anyone wondered about my dedication to journalism, it was now official.

Hildy Biddle, Undercover Babysitter.

I sat under a folding table playing castle with Missy

Grimes. She was the princess, I was her lady-in-waiting, and the bad news was that several fire-breathing dragons had surrounded the castle and only one of us (Missy) was brave enough to fight them.

Missy raised a spatula and screamed, "I'll waste some of you before you bring me down!"

Mrs. Grimes had warned me that Missy's father let her watch violent movies.

I was trying to find a comfortable way to kneel. "Well, Princess—methinks you scared the dragons away."

"They're still out there," Missy said. "I can smell them." She sniffed the air. "They smell like bad milk."

My back was close to spasming. "I've heard that dragons leave the bad-milk smell when they're retreating."

She shook her head. "That's wrong. My daddy is going to come to rescue us."

"That's good." I handed her a wand covered with sparkling stars. "I was told, Princess, that this wand will scare off the dragons."

That was wrong, too.

"Listen, Missy. Do you remember when you and your class were at my orchard?"

"Shhhh. They can hear you."

I whispered, "When you were at the orchard, you mentioned seeing something big. Huge, even."

She nodded, waved the wand around.

"Was that a dragon you saw?"

"No."

"What was it?"

"It was a ghost." She screamed, "Dragons, get ready to die!"

"Where did you see the ghost?"

"At the bad house."

"Where is that?"

"The one that killed the little girl."

Careful. "What were you doing there?"

She looked down. "I was riding my bike and I got lost."

"Was your mother with you?"

"Yes."

I decided not to ask how you get lost in your hometown when your mother's with you. "Missy, what happened after you saw the ghost?"

"I got scared."

"I bet."

She crawled out from under the folding table. I followed. She ran up to her room and handed me a well-worn copy of *The Brave Little Chipmunk*.

"You read it to me, Hildy, because I'm supposed to hear it when I get afraid."

"Okay. I'm sorry if anything I said—"

"Read it to me! Read it to me!"

I started reading about Chappy Chipmunk, who overcame an evil badger who had it in for small animals. The book ended with Chappy, surrounded by a grateful chipmunk community, saying her closing line.

"Anything is possible when you have a true heart."

Missy shouted the last line with feeling. I remembered reading this to her when I babysat last year.

Missy looked in the mirror, tossed her hair, and smiled. "I'm famous."

"Are you the girl they wrote about in the paper?"

She nodded. "And Daddy is very worried, and he's coming to save me all the way from Atlanta."

She jumped on her pink bed, burrowed among the stuffed animals, and grinned.

Baker was out of town for the next few days.

I was sitting in Tanisha's kitchen, eating spicy orange beef, which her mother made when she needed to feel good about the world. Mrs. Bass was a counselor at the middle school and was making a lot of spicy orange beef these days. It was rich and dense with just enough sweetness. Pookie was curled up in her dog bed.

"So what do I do about Missy?" I asked Tanisha.

We'd already discarded the idea of doing a blog about her under an assumed name.

"I think you should write down everything about Missy that you remember, Hildy."

"That will take decades," I mentioned.

"She's only six."

I put my head in my hands. Where do I start?

Tanisha took out a yellow pad and started writing. "Her dad lets her watch violent movies. Getting scared and exaggerating is the way to get her parents' attention."

"Her parents' divorce has been hard on her," I added.

Tanisha wrote that down, too. "That doesn't mean she should make the front page."

I shrugged. "She already has, though, and it's selling newspapers! You've seen how *The Bee* is getting bigger with every issue. They've got so many ads!"

"Ads," Tanisha said, "not content."

I sighed. "They're successful, Tanisha, and that makes them powerful."

"You're saying that Pen Piedmont has more power than the truth because he's got a lot of ads?"

"No! I'm saying that—"

Tanisha pressed in. "You're saying that because of his power he gets to exploit kids without being challenged? *Shouldn't someone challenge him?*"

Pookie barked.

I looked at the photo of Martin Luther King Jr. that hung on the wall. Tanisha's grandfather marched with Dr. King during the civil rights demonstrations in the sixties. Dr. King had signed the photo *To Edmer Bass, Who walked the miles for peace and justice.*

It's hard to wimp out sitting in this kitchen.

Tanisha and I were in town, standing by the offices of *The Bee*, trying to run into Pen Piedmont as though it was a random occurrence. Madame Zobek's psychic studio was next door. I saw Jackie Jowrey, Elizabeth's friend who was running for Homecoming Queen, come out the studio door. She looked at me and smiled nervously. A few more people walked inside.

I looked at Tanisha, who was infused with purpose. "Tell me again why we're doing this," I insisted.

"We're facing down the bully, Hildy. We're going to tell him we know that he's lying. We're going to draw our line in the sand."

"I'd rather write an article."

Pinky Sandusky marched up to *The Bee*'s office holding an envelope.

"Hi, Mrs. Sandusky."

"Hello, yourself. I'm making my afternoon delivery. Piedmont's not printing my letters to the editor, so I bring one to him every day. I have a right for my voice to be heard!"

I smiled. "If you send me a copy of the letter, I'll see if we can run it in *The Core*."

She nodded and pushed through the door.

Then, Sheriff Metcalf walked by. He glanced at Madame Zobek's studio. "What are you doing here, Hildy?"

"Waiting for someone."

Tanisha pointed to the parking lot. "Let's wait there."

We hurried across the street. It was easy to spot Piedmont's black SUV because of the license plate.

MYTPEN

How mighty was his pen, anyway?

Lev pulled up in his red VW.

"Vant a ride, my dears?" He said it like Dracula. "My carriage is at your service." He lowered his voice. "I could take you to my decaying castle."

Nooooooo . . . .

Lev leaned out the window, flashing a brilliant smile. "Look, Hildy, you know homecoming's coming up, and I'm a very good dancer."

Last year we won the dance contest at homecoming.

"And I'd *really* like to go with you." Lev, like Dracula, oozed charm.

I felt this pent-up desire to say yes just to win the dance contest again.

Thankfully, Tanisha cleared her throat and touched her red sweater. Red stood for "Danger." That broke the spell.

Only God knew how many times Lev had cheated on me, and God wasn't telling.

"I'm busy," I croaked out.

He adjusted his rearview mirror. "Too bad. I bid you farewell." And off he drove.

I grabbed Tanisha's arm. "I almost cracked."

"But you didn't." She put on sunglasses. I did, too. We stood there.

Next, Zack drove up. I'm telling you, it's impossible to hide in Banesville.

He looked at us, amused. "What are you guys doing?"

"Waiting for Piedmont," we said in unison.

He parked his car and joined us.

Zack stood close to me. I don't know why, but I moved just a little closer. Our arms touched. Tanisha pointed to her black boots. Black stood for "What's going on?"

Nothing's going on, I mouthed.

"I've been doing some research on fake psychics," Zack told us. "In this one town the bank teller called the sheriff because suddenly people were taking all this cash out of their accounts. Turns out they were giving it to this psychic who had five aliases."

I turned to Zack. "Really?"

"Con artists know how to spot vulnerabilities very quickly in people," he added. "That's how they operate."

"Speak of the devil," Tanisha said.

Mighty Pen himself was walking toward the lot.

"Look normal," I whispered.

"Too late for that," Tanisha muttered.

Piedmont walked more slowly as he saw us.

"Hi, Mr. Piedmont," we all said together.

"Cute act you've got." He pressed his key chain, un-locking the SUV.

I took off my sunglasses. "That article on the girl see-ing the ghost is really something," I mentioned.

No eye contact. "We're proud of the reporting."

"I babysit for Missy Grimes," I added.

His neck muscles tensed. "Who?"

"Missy Grimes," I repeated. "The local girl who said she saw a ghost. I need to tell you, she's got a wild imagination."

107

"We're not releasing the identity of the girl. But I can assure you she's been scared and our story is on the level."

"Mr. Piedmont, I don't believe your story is accurate."

"*My* stories are always accurate!" Two women had stopped to listen. Seeing them, Piedmont went folksy. "The world needs stories. That's how we learn. The news business is about finding those stories and bringing them to the people."

The two women nodded and walked to their car.

He climbed into the SUV and drove off too fast.

I shouted after him, "The news business is about reporting true stories—not making them up!"

Chapter 12

✣✣✣✣✣✣✣✣✣✣✣✣✣✣✣✣✣✣✣✣✣✣✣✣✣✣✣✣✣✣✣✣✣✣✣✣✣

"It's a big news day, you guys." Darrell walked into Room 67B, waving a sheet of paper. "The coroner's report is back on Lupo. You're not going to believe this. He died of natural causes—a heart attack."

What?

"How is that possible?" Elizabeth demanded.

"He wasn't choked, shot, poisoned, knifed, hit, run over, or beat up. The guy was overweight and out of shape. He had a heart attack." Darrell leaned against the table. "And the other piece of news is that Houston Bule was released on bail."

"When?" I demanded.

"This morning."

"So there wasn't a murder?" Elizabeth asked.

"No." Darrell laughed. "Piedmont is going to have to change his story."

"He's good at that, though," T.R. said.

"*Get ready*," Baker warned, walking in the door. "Piedmont's invested a lot of ink in a murder. He's going to hit back hard."

Baker was right. *The Bee* came roaring into the newsstands.

SCARED TO DEATH!

The front-page article talked about how seeing a terrifying ghost could cause a heart attack in just about anybody. There was an "interview" with a cardiac specialist who said that he had seen several patients who'd had heart attacks due to paranormal sightings.

Madame Zobek's column took up all of page three.

"I, myself," she wrote, "have almost been propelled into shock by the things I have seen in the other world. It is only because of my experience and my ability to work with these dark forces that I am here with you today and able to offer my assistance. We must not look the other way, for there are those who do not understand the power of these close encounters. Clearly, the ghost of Clarence Ludlow is a dangerous presence . . ."

That sent Baker Polton into orbit, which isn't easy in a closet-sized room. He threw *The Bee* on the floor and hollered, "What are we about at this paper?"

T.R., Lev, Tanisha, Elizabeth, and I looked to Darrell.

"News?" Darrell replied hopefully.

"For whom?" Baker yelled.

"Um, the high school?"

"Why?"

"Well, because . . ." Darrell's eyes darted around the windowless office. "We're in high school?"

"We've got a bozo who likes rubbing fear and lies in people's faces. He's the only media source in town except us. Who are we writing for?"

Elizabeth waved her hand emotionally. "The American people!"

Baker clasped his brow. "Let's narrow that."

Darrell stood. "We're writing for the community."

"And they deserve the facts," Baker warned. "Don't ever forget it."

Late afternoon shadows crept across the Ludlow lawn. Several crows caw-cawed from a gnarled crab apple tree in the front yard. It had died long ago but still stood, leafless and hollow. In apple country, a dead, fruitless tree makes people nervous. We don't want to look at a tree that can't produce.

Everything we work for comes under one heading: being fruitful.

This house wasn't producing much except fear.

A squirrel crawled across the iron fence, looked at the house, and ran the other way.

A strange assortment of stones, beer cans, and candles was piled on the Ludlow front porch.

A few cars drove slowly down the street with their windows up.

A woman in a long black dress stood by the Ludlow gate, swaying back and forth.

"Hi."

I jumped.

"Sorry, Hildy." It was Zack. He was wearing a brown turtleneck and jeans. He looked good. I'd asked him to meet me there.

"So," he said, "what are we doing?"

"I'm trying to figure something out and I thought you could help me. I want to know how a scientist would prove or deny all the stories surrounding this house."

He thought about that. "Well, like reporters, scientists ask questions. We call it scientific inquiry. So in this case the first question might be: Is there a ghost making the Ludlow house a dangerous place? If so, then how do we prove that?"

"Eyewitnesses . . . ," I mentioned.

"If they're reliable and what they've seen can be proved."

The swaying woman by the gate was singing now. She didn't shout *reliable*.

Pinky Sandusky and two old women walked up to us wearing red sweatshirts that read ELDERS AGAINST EVIL. I tried not to laugh.

"Keep talking, young man," Pinky ordered.

Zack hid a smile. "People can say they've seen all kinds of things—sixteen planets, flying pigs, you name it. But the basis of science is that the universe has an order to it. Scientists try to find patterns that will answer questions and confirm or deny a theory."

"And that means what for Farnsworth Road?" another of the Elders Against Evil demanded.

Zack folded his arms. "It means there needs to be further observation and documentation for any claim about a ghost to be taken seriously."

"How do we get that?" Pinky demanded.

"I guess someone needs to watch the house day and night and record what they see," Zack explained.

"That sounds like a big job," Pinky observed.

"It would be, yes."

"Not a job for a pushover," Pinky added.

"A pushover couldn't begin to handle this," Zack agreed.

The Elders Against Evil folded their arms and nodded.

Suddenly, the sky went dark and a strong wind blew down the street. A dead tree branch from the Ludlow yard crashed to the ground.

The elders looked at each other. I grabbed Zack's arm.

"That's a pattern," Pinky told him. "Branches falling. What do you call *that*?"

"Gravity," Zack offered.

She considered that, then pointed to the pile of rocks and candles on the porch. "We've got some visitors making this property their shrine. We've got ghost hunters prowling the street; that Zobek woman floating around like she's a tour guide." Pinky turned to the elders. "Well, girls, we've been looking for a community project."

"This beats the beans out of quilting," another elder said.

Pinky shouted, "Are we going to take this street back or what?"

"Let's do it!" They clapped their hands like football players leaving a huddle and headed toward her house, real slow.

I watched the swaying woman get in her car and drive away. That left Zack and me alone.

Honestly, I wanted to leave, too. I've never been a fan of dark, encroaching shadows.

Finally Zack said, "Hildy, I need to tell you something."

"What?"

He cleared his throat. "I've never said this to a girl before."

I bit my lip, waiting.

"Well . . ." He looked down. "I'm not sure how to say

this." He took a deep breath and announced, "I really like fighting evil with you."

He went back to watching the house.

A few crows squawked from the dead tree.

"I like fighting evil with you, too," I actually muttered.

Chapter 13

✿❖✿❖✿❖✿❖✿❖✿❖✿❖✿❖✿❖✿❖✿❖✿❖✿❖✿❖✿❖✿❖✿❖✿❖✿❖

MURDEROUS GHOST WAITING FOR NEXT VICTIM

GHOST SIGHTINGS UP 50%

BANESVILLE ON RED ALERT

Collectively, the staff of *The Core* was gagging at *The Bee*'s latest edition.

Zack had come into room 67B while we were looking at Tanisha's spooky photo of three weird people getting out of a van in front of the Ludlow house—the van had GHOST CHASERS painted on the side.

"Have any of you seen a ghost?" Zack asked us.

That didn't seem like a question he'd ask, although trying to figure him out was a mystery.

"Because if all the ghost sightings are real," he continued, "don't you think at least one of us would have seen one or known someone who did?"

"Up fifty percent means half the town would have seen one," Lev challenged.

"The percentage makes it sound like that," Zack agreed, "but you've got to ask, fifty percent up from what? If four people said they saw a ghost, a fifty-percent increase would mean only two more people saw one. That's the trick. Fearmongers do it all the time."

Lev was silent as Baker wrote FEARMONGERS on the whiteboard.

Elizabeth raised her hand. "What's a monger?"

"One who sells something," Baker offered. "A fishmonger sells fish. A fearmonger—"

"Sells fear," Elizabeth whispered.

Baker circled FEARMONGERS. "This is a big thing to fight."

"We need our own data," Zack insisted.

Baker pointed at him. "Keep talking."

"I think we need to test what they say."

"Do you know how to do that?" Darrell asked him.

Hands in his pockets, Zack said, "Yeah."

Darrell thought about that. "Look, Zack, would you like to work on the paper? We could really use someone like you."

Zack shook his head. "I'm not a good writer."

"Neither am I, but they let me write," Elizabeth offered.

"You could be the research manager," Baker suggested.

"I think I'd rather just help," Zack muttered. He looked at me when he said it.

Darrell walked toward Zack and stuck out his hand. "It's settled then. We need help. Welcome to *The Core*."

WHAT HAVE YOU SEEN?
PLEASE TAKE PART IN
A SPECIAL *CORE* SURVEY

Posters went up all over the school. *E-mail us, call us, stop us in the hall.* It wasn't easy coming up with the questions. Zack said we had to ask ones that would give us direct answers.

Have you . . .
Seen a ghost?
Heard a ghost?
Seen something spooky?
Heard something spooky?
Witnessed a crime?
Committed a crime?
Called the police or fire department?
Wish you'd called (see above)?
Don't get what all the excitement is about—you haven't seen or heard anything?

Zack was in charge of tabulating the responses. Some

responses were beyond tabulation. Those went into a box marked DISGUSTING AND DERANGED.

"How long before we get the results?" I asked Zack.

"A few days. I want to get back as many surveys as I can."

"How," Baker Polton asked, "can you tell if a source is reliable?"

Zack, Lev, T.R., Tanisha, Darrell, Elizabeth, and I looked at each other.

We were sitting in the back room at Minska's, at the big round table, feeling like prisoners who had been set free. Baker had made an executive decision. We were having a few staff lunches off-site, away from *that room*.

"It's someone who's trustworthy?" I offered.

Baker took a bite of his grilled panini sandwich. "But how do you know someone is trustworthy?"

I glanced at Lev, who was checking his phone messages, not paying attention.

"By what they do?" I asked.

T.R. added, "By what they say?"

Baker sat there chewing. "Are you with us, Radner, or would you like to leave?"

"Sorry." Lev put his phone away.

"With any source, you have to ask yourself—would this person be making up a story to impress people?"

I went through my list in my head. Missy was the only questionable one.

"Now, how do you get your reliable sources to go on the record?"

Elizabeth raised her hand. "We say how important it is for responsible people to come forward during this time when there's so much happening that could be false."

Baker was impressed. "Very good. But what if that doesn't work?"

No one answered.

Baker sipped his latte. "Always remember, people change. One day they might not talk, the next day they might. That's why you keep going back, asking questions. I think a good approach could be to ask: What do you think of the article in *The Bee*? What do you wish people in town understood about what's going on? If you get answers, your follow-up is what?"

"'It would help the town if you'd go on the record,'" I said.

"Now you're thinking." He almost looked happy.

Baker walked over to the wall and studied a picture of Pope John Paul II addressing the crowds in Poland.

"I remember this day," he told us. "I was just a kid. My mother's family is half Polish. My grandmother told me the pope's words sparked the revolution. You know what he said?" He read from the plaque. "'The future of Poland will depend on how many people are mature enough to be nonconformists.' Let me tell you something. The future of the world still rests on that."

Minska stood in the doorway. "I was there when he

120

spoke. I'd never seen so many people—all of us hungry for change. My father told me, 'Today our new history begins.'"

"This is quite a place you've got here," Baker said.

She smiled. "Food and revolution—that's what I know about."

Elizabeth gushed, "I swear, Hildy, when we were at Minska's, I felt like we were all being called to this greater thing that I don't understand yet, but somehow it's right out front for us to grab. It was just way so inspiring. Do you know what I mean?"

"Kind of."

"I mean, Minska has lived through history!"

"We're living through history, too."

"I never thought of that." Elizabeth was wearing black leggings and a beaded T-shirt that read CUTIE. "But I've been thinking about the girl and ghost and sources. Roddy's sister Ann is a nurse in the ER. If that girl had been brought in, she might have some information." Roddy is Elizabeth's boyfriend, loyal beyond words.

"That's a great idea."

"So, get over there, Hildy!"

"It's your idea, Elizabeth. You want to come?"

She bounded up, grinning.

We were in the hospital cafeteria with Ann. "You understand I can't give you names," she said.

121

"Oh, we totally do," said Elizabeth. She gives up fast.

"You understand that I'd prefer if you'd not use my name," Ann said quietly.

I glanced at Elizabeth and said, "Could you tell us what you can?"

"A little girl was brought in around three on that day. She had hurt her elbow after falling off her bike in front of the Ludlow house. The elbow needed a few stitches. That's all."

"That's all?" I asked. "Did she mention seeing a ghost?"

"No."

"Could there have been another girl who was injured?"

"I was here all day."

"Could the girl *The Bee* mentioned have gone to another hospital?"

"The closest hospital is thirty miles away."

"Was her mother with her?" Elizabeth asked.

"Yes."

I leaned forward. "What was she like?"

"She was a little worried, but none of this was in any way remarkable."

"What do you think of that article in *The Bee*?" I asked.

Ann sipped her tea. "I think it's highly inaccurate."

"Could I quote you?" I asked. "Because this could—"

She shook her head. "I want to help, but I'm not sure

how the administration would feel about it." She dipped her tea bag up and down in the mug.

I sure wished Baker was here.

"Your name would help us," I tried again, "because—"

"I *can't*."

"We don't want you to get in trouble," Elizabeth said gently. "We so appreciate you telling us this much. We want to write the truth and you're helping us find it."

I wrote my number down, tore off the sheet, and handed it to her. "If you remember anything else, Ann, would you let us know?"

She looked at the paper, put it in her pocket. "Look, you girls are doing a good thing. I've got to get back to work."

"I think we let her off the hook too easily, Elizabeth!" I backed the truck out of the parking lot fast to make the point.

Elizabeth sat there with her hands folded.

"We're never going to get to the heart of this thing if people won't go on the record!"

Elizabeth hung her head and didn't say anything. It's hard to fight with a person who doesn't fight back.

A dark car pulled up alongside ours. Madame Zobek was driving. She smiled at us a little longer than was comfortable. Then she drove off.

"She gives me the creeps," I said, turning down our street.

"I think she's interesting. She knows things, Hildy."
Elizabeth's voice rose. "Jackie told me she's amazing."

My antenna went up. Elizabeth and Jackie were spending more time together in and out of school.

"Jackie said her entire psyche was exploding when she went to Madame Zobek," Elizabeth added.

"I like my psyche in one piece."

"You would, Hildy."

I pulled into our driveway. I didn't like how Elizabeth was sounding. I turned to her.

"Elizabeth, you're not seeing Madame Zobek, right?"

"Of course not," she said.

"Good, because that would be really dumb."

She looked at me sweetly. "I'm not dumb."

"I know. But sometimes you can be kind of impressionable, and I don't mean that as—"

"I resent that!" She climbed out of the truck fast, slammed the door, and ran into the house.

Chapter 14

✥✥✥✥✥✥✥✥✥✥✥✥✥✥✥✥✥✥✥✥✥✥✥✥✥✥✥✥✥✥✥✥✥

LOCAL GIRL TRAUMATIZED AFTER SEEING GHOST CHILD PROCLAIMS, "I HAVE A TRUE HEART!"

The local girl who was propelled off her bike after seeing a ghostly presence at the Ludlow estate said yesterday, "I can't sleep at night, I'm so scared. I hope the town will do something about this because children are in danger. I would never lie about something like that. I have a true heart." The girl was hospitalized after the accident and released to her mother's care. "I've never seen her like this," the mother said. "I know this all seems crazy, but my daughter wouldn't make up something like this up."

I have a true heart—that was the chipmunk's line in Missy Grimes's book.

And *The Bee* had in-depth coverage of the Ludlow place, including interviews with unidentified sources "too afraid to come forward."

It's a funny thing how fear grows. It moves like a virus, infecting person after person.

There wasn't any medicine to stop the epidemic, either.

Children were having nightmares about the killer ghost; some were afraid to leave their houses and come to school.

One kindergarten teacher stopped taking her students out to recess because several of them said they saw a bad ghost behind a tree on the playground.

I remembered my long year fighting fear in eighth grade after Dad died.

"Everybody's afraid of something," Gwen, my therapist, told me back then. "And fear isn't always a bad thing, Hildy. It can alert us to real danger." The operative word, Gwen said, was *real*, not imagined.

Imagined fears are hard to nail down. For a while I was afraid every time my mom would go out that she'd get in a car accident and never come back. I was afraid that I'd never be happy again, I'd always be crying. I was scared that I had a weak heart like my dad and I'd die at thirty-eight just like he did.

I was in my bedroom. I slid open my mirrored closet door and pushed through clothes to the old file cabinet. I pulled out an article Dad wrote about how the family of a murdered policeman was trying to cope with the loss.

The chair where Larry Olen used to sit is empty now. It sits as it always did by the bookcase filled with history books, sits as a symbol of loss, and something the family can't quite discard. "We've tried moving it into the other room," said Mary, his widow, "but it doesn't seem right there. I guess we just need to have this memory of him, even though it's hard."

I looked at Dad's old hiking boots that I kept near my bed. We were always hiking in the woods together.

The boots that Mitch Biddle used to wear are empty now. They sit in the corner of his only daughter's room, sit as a symbol of an important life being taken too soon.

MacIntosh padded over and the sniffed the boots.

"I miss him, too, Mac."

MacIntosh sat by the boots. I went over, kicked off my shoes, put my feet in Dad's big boots, and stood there.

I couldn't exactly fill his shoes, but there was enough of him in my heart that shoe size didn't matter. I clunked over to my desk, opened my laptop, and wrote,

We have nothing to fear but fear itself.

FDR said that during World War II.

I wondered if some kind of war was trying to break out in Banesville.

127

❖❖❖

"Are you afraid to go out? Are you afraid to stay inside? Safety First has a line of home and personal security devices to make you feel safer. Stay on the line and one of our representatives will assist you."

Nan got the call and hung up, but lots of residents didn't. One by one people began ordering extra-loud house alarms, mace, nightsticks.

Banesville's citizens were becoming alarmed and armed.

The Bee had a new front-page section called "The Terror Grows."

Random aggression, they assured us, *was breaking out everywhere.*

At Jethro's Gym: *A bodybuilder erupted in rage at a man who had taken his dumbbell by mistake. The man said he was pushed and suffered bruises to his hand. The bodybuilder is still at large.*

At Lull's Cheap Gas: *A shoving contest over a gasoline pump erupted in violence.*

At the middle school: *Lunch money was stolen from students on Thursday, prompting worried parents to ask, "Are our schools safe?"*

I called Tanisha's mom, the middle school counselor, and asked her if she knew about the stolen lunch money.

Mrs. Bass was furious about *The Bee's* coverage: "No money was stolen, Hildy. One kid dropped a few quarters, another grabbed them, and he was ordered by a teacher to give the money back. Everyone had lunch! I think par-

128

ents in town should be worried, but not about this school. They should be worried about the irresponsible journalism printed in *The Bee!*"

"Can I quote you, Mrs. Bass?"

"You bet!"

It was all we could do to try and set the record straight. Staying ahead of scare tactics is a full-time job.

Elsewhere around town, Crescent Furl at A to Z Convenience now stocked a complete line of Safety First products, including the Make My Day Pepper Spray Key Chain, which, she said, was flying off the shelves.

The Elders Against Evil dragged their lawn chairs in front of the Ludlow house and started "observation shifts," peering through binoculars.

"Have you seen anything?" I asked Pinky.

She checked her observation shift report. "A tour bus, a plumber, six dogs, the mailman."

"No ghosts?" I asked her.

"Not a one."

"What's going on with you and Zack?" Tanisha turned her Honda onto Red Road and drove toward the high school. "And don't say 'nothing,' Hildy, because that's not going to cut it. You know what I'm talking about."

"He's the research director."

She drove past a FOR SALE sign for one of the orchards that now said SOLD. "He's been around long before that. Tell me. And by the way, you're blushing."

"I don't blush," I said. "And keep your eyes on the road."

"I'm the one who doesn't blush, girl!" We started laughing. "You do not have the right to remain silent about this issue," she insisted. "You like him, don't you?" She turned into the parking lot and avoided the first of three huge potholes.

"I don't know."

"Hildy, he's not a Lev or a Nathan."

"He's a scientist."

"*And?*"

I didn't want to talk about this. "He's helpful."

"*And?*"

"Brainy guys are helpful."

"And your relationship is *what?*"

"It's complicated," I said.

"I'm going to need more than that, Hildy."

Okay, you asked for it. "Zack and I fight evil together."

That stunned her to silence.

Colorful brochures started appearing around the high school—in the cafeteria, on seats in the library, on car and truck windshields in the parking lot. The cover had a close-up of a girl's big blue eyes; across the top in curlicue writing were the words

A New Look at Bonnie Sue Bomgartner

Inside, the brochure showed Bonnie Sue's most meaningful moments—looking gorgeous while working at the St. Claire soup kitchen, looking stunning while collecting canned goods for the poor, looking perfect as a baby, toddler, kindergartner, etc.

Bonnie Sue breezed past me in the hall, waving hello like we were close friends. She was campaigning round the clock for people to vote for her as Homecoming Queen.

The other contestants, Lacey, Chelsea, and Jackie, didn't have Bonnie Sue's big-pocket funding. As president of the horticulture club, Lacey tended the apple trees on the school property and ran programs that brought inner-city kids to the country to learn about rural life. She didn't honk her horn about it, she just did it. Lacey said that if elected, she was coming to the dance alone, since she didn't have a boyfriend and she didn't believe in dredging one up for show. Every unattached student threw her their support.

I walked to the Student Center and grabbed a ballot from the back table.

If you don't vote, your voice won't be heard.

I skipped Bonnie Sue Bomgartner's name and put a fat X by Lacey Horton.

I dropped my ballot in the box and noticed my two former boyfriends, Nathan and Lev, watching me. My relationship failures crashed in like waves.

Finding a good boyfriend was like trying to find a ghost.

Or Sallie Miner's father. I'd finally drummed up the

courage to start calling the eleven Lawrence Miners on the list I'd compiled from the Miami phone book. I'd called ten names and hadn't found him. The three men I'd spoken to weren't very friendly. I left messages for the others; no one called me back.

I went to *The Core*'s office and called the last Lawrence Miner on my list, number eleven.

"Hello," a man answered.

"Is this the home of Lawrence Miner?" I asked into the phone, trying not to sound like a telemarketer.

"Yes," the man said hesitantly into the phone.

"Mr. Miner?"

"Who is this?"

"This is Hildy Biddle, sir. I live in Banesville, New York."

"Mitch Biddle's girl?"

"*Yes.*"

"God, I haven't talked to anyone from Banesville for years."

I found him!

"How is your dad doing?" he asked.

"Oh . . ." I sighed. "He's not doing so well, Mr. Miner. He died a few years ago."

Silence, then, "I'm so sorry, Hildy. Your dad was a great guy."

I bit my lip. "I guess you and I have losing someone we love in common."

"I guess we do," he said sadly.

132

I told him why I was calling, told him what had been happening in town. "I don't want to intrude in any way, Mr. Miner. I can understand if you wouldn't want to talk about Sallie."

"I do, though, Hildy. It would help me. You know Sallie had an amazing love for make-believe. She was a sensitive girl—it was hard on her, she felt different from the other kids. I don't know how she first heard about the Ludlow stories, maybe at school. But she just zeroed in on that like there was a ghost who was personally out to get her. She had nightmares; she'd come home crying. We had her see a doctor and things seemed to settle down . . ." He stopped talking.

I was writing like mad. I asked the big question. "Do you think she saw a ghost the day of the accident?"

"She never told me that. Her mother and I were in the hospital with her round the clock for three days. A nurse was the one who told that story."

"A nurse? Do you know the nurse's name?"

"No. The story just spread all over town. I think people were trying to make sense of such a tragedy, trying to find something to pin it on. Do you know what I mean?"

"When people are scared, they look for something to blame," I said, remembering what Eaton Ebbers had told me.

"Exactly!" He sighed. "Her mother and I—this thing split us apart. We didn't have the strength to talk to people. We should have gone someplace to heal. We didn't do that. Your dad came by so often to talk with me and listen. He helped me more than I know how to say."

That so touched me. "Dad was a good listener." I was writing as fast as I could. I had one more big question. I took a huge breath. "Mr. Miner, could I quote you?"

"Absolutely."

"*Thank you.*"

"No. Thank *you*, Hildy. Your dad would be so proud of you."

I sat there and let the tears come.

"These are direct quotes?" Baker asked me. He was sitting at the desk, drinking coffee.

"Yes."

"No doubt?"

"None."

"Mr. Miner gave you permission to use his name?"

"Yes."

He deleted my phrase *in an emotionally charged interview* and pushed the piggy bank close.

I dropped in dimes, grumbling that it *was* emotionally charged.

He handed the copy back to me. "Good work." The left side of his mouth curled up, which was how Baker smiled. "*Run it.*"

I called it "Remembering Sallie," and people read it.

Really read it.

Kids stopped me in the hall.

Minska asked for extra issues to have at the cash register.

Sheriff Metcalf called me at home, saying it was a fine job.

I mailed a copy to Mr. Miner in Miami, hoping he'd like it.

It still didn't get me a date to homecoming, but Tanisha, always the forward thinker, had ideas about that.

"We're both going to miss the dance, Hildy, so let me lay this out for you. I checked the National Weather Service and we're supposed to get high winds and rain Saturday night, which would mean if we went we'd be miserable and wet. I also checked the Centers for Disease Control website and it looks like people are getting the flu early this year and the shots won't be ready until November, if at all. Just think of the bacteria crawling on the food table. We'd be taking our lives in our hands. Also, that week in October is usually when cold season starts, so we'd be close-up to those germs, too." She nuzzled Pookie and said, "We don't know how good we've got it."

For some reason that helped.

As the election for Homecoming Queen drew closer, Elizabeth was acting strangely. She was spending lots of time in her room, and she didn't want to pet MacIntosh because she said he might have germs.

"Are you okay?" I asked her. She was standing in the

clearing in the orchard, looking at the rust-colored sunset that seemed painted across the sky.

"I know who's going to be the Homecoming Queen," Elizabeth told me.

"Bonnie Sue, probably," I said. All the popular kids were handing out her brochures. "Have you seen the stickers? 'Bonnie Sue, we love you!'" I groaned.

Elizabeth laughed happily. "Jackie's going to win."

As far I knew Jackie didn't really stand a chance. Every thinking person in school was voting for Lacey, but whether she could beat Bonnie Sue's heavily financed campaign was unclear.

"It's a done deal, Hildy," Elizabeth assured me. "Jackie's got it."

"What are you talking about?"

Elizabeth kept staring at the sunset that was being swallowed up by the night. "Madame Zobek told Jackie she was going to win."

I stared at her. "You don't really believe Madame Zobek's for real, do you?"

Elizabeth kept looking at the sky. "There are things in this world that are greater than we know, Hildy."

"Have you gone to see Madame Zobek?" I demanded.

Elizabeth shook her soft blond curls. "Of course not!" She walked quickly away.

I think that was the first time Elizabeth ever lied to me. Something spooky seemed to hover in the air.

Chapter 15

Homecoming fever was everywhere. It was a welcome relief, too, from the creeping, crawling hype around the Ludlow house.

"You know what I love about this school?" Mr. Grasso shouted from the makeshift stage in the cafeteria. He gazed proudly at the GO BEASTS! sports banner and said, "We've got it where it counts! We don't have the newest facilities, we don't have the fanciest uniforms, but we've got heart! I'm calling on every one of you to rally strong for our teams during Spirit Week! Let's cheer the Beasts on to homecoming victory!"

Among Beasts fans, Tanisha's dog Pookie was the only true believer. She came to every pep rally and jumped with the cheerleaders. She ran across the football field during practice in her navy-and-orange GO BEASTS! sweatshirt.

Pookie also learned to pee on *The Bee*'s special editions.

"Right here, baby." Tanisha pointed to the front-page article and Pookie let loose on badly written copy:

"The living room is the most haunted place," said an undisclosed source who supposedly had been inside the Ludlow house. "And by the fireplace I could feel the spirit of Mrs. Ludlow the most. Sometimes I could hear her crying. Once I asked if there was anything I could do to help, and suddenly something tried to push me on the floor! I ran out of there fast, and when I got home, I had black-and-blue marks on my back!"

I'm sorry, this isn't journalism.

But it got into the atmosphere just the same.

Even into Spirit Week at Banesville High. Someone added an E and O to all the Spirit Week posters, changing SPIRIT to ESPIRITO, which means "ghost" in Spanish.

The Bee had its own Spirit Week celebration.

"Homecoming isn't just for high school," wrote Madame Zobek. *"Homecoming has at its root a deeper dimension. I sense that many spirits of the dead will find their way home to Banesville at the beckoning of the ghosts now gathered on Farnsworth Road."*

I went over to Farnsworth Road to see what Pinky Sandusky had to say about that. The leaves were changing to brilliant reds and deep yellows, but nothing, not even autumn's beauty, could make the Ludlow house look respectable.

She showed me her 24/7 time chart of everything observed.

Assorted birds.

Assorted weirdos.

No ghosts, however.

"How long have you and your friends been watching the property?" I asked her.

"Close to three weeks."

"And what do you think your findings mean?"

"I have no proof whatsoever that any kind of ghost resides on this property."

"Can I quote you?"

"Honey, you can stick my words on a bumper sticker."

Home.

I was standing outside Elizabeth's room. The door was shut; I knocked on it.

"It's me," I said.

"Just a minute," Elizabeth said nervously.

It sounded like she was putting things away. I never do this, but I walked in anyway.

There was a tray on the bed with photos of her mother in antique frames; Elizabeth and her mom looked so much alike. Next to the photos were candles. I could tell they'd just been blown out—the wicks were smoking.

"What are you doing?" I asked.

Her heart-shaped face was furious. "Who gave you permission, Hildy, to just barge in here?"

"What are you doing?" I asked again.

Tears came to Elizabeth's eyes. She gathered up the

photographs of her mother. There was a big pile of money on her dresser, too.

"What's the money for, Elizabeth?"

"Leave me alone, Hildy."

"Are you seeing Madame Zobek?" I persisted.

"No! I already told you! Leave me alone!"

"Sorry, I can't do that." I sat on her bed. "What's going on?"

Elizabeth's hands started shaking. She dropped to her knees on the hooked rug, crying.

"I only went to her two times, Hildy. She said my mother wanted to talk with me, but something was preventing it . . ."

"Madame Zobek told you this?"

She nodded, weeping.

"What else did she tell you?"

"She said that there were special candles she could get me that would help set Mom's spirit free so she could come to me."

I looked at her bed. "Are those the candles?"

She bit her lip; nodded.

"How much are you paying her?"

"Not that much."

I looked at the money on her dresser. Elizabeth had sponge painted that dresser in white and silver last year. It was beautiful.

"And what is she charging for the candles?"

"A hundred dollars, okay? But she gave me the special sale price and—"

"You gave some woman in a cape a hundred dollars!"

"You weren't there, Hildy. I was. You didn't hear her— I did. You knew your father, I never knew my mother, and if she's trying to get back to give me a message, I'm going to spend everything I've got to hear her!" She threw a lace pillow across the room.

I stood on the porch, trying to figure out what to do. I could see my breath in the air, floating like a wisp.

I had to tell, I knew that.

I hated having to do it.

When Elizabeth and I were younger, I used to tease her that she was part apple because her emotions bruised so easily. I didn't want her to get hurt in any way.

Felix had gone to bed early. Nan and Mom were at an Apple Alliance meeting.

Nan was the one who needed to talk to Elizabeth. Nan understood her gentleness better than anyone.

It was 10:45 when Mom and Nan walked through the door, exhausted. Apple Alliance meetings are grueling.

Mom flopped into the floral chair by the fireplace. "Why do I do this?" she asked me.

"To make the world safe for apple buyers everywhere," I reminded her.

Nan took off her glasses and rubbed her eyes. "Dear

Lord, forgive me, but when Eve Lundquist starts talking about expanding the market for fruit, she just goes on forever."

"I need to talk to you both about something important."

Nan kicked off her clodhoppers. "Go ahead, darlin'."

I told them about Elizabeth, the money, and what Zack had found out about fake psychics.

Nan stood up. "We're stopping this before it goes any further. Is Felix awake?"

"He went to bed."

Nan went to wake him up.

Mom shook out her ponytail. "You did the right thing telling us, Hildy."

Then why did I feel like an informant? Because Elizabeth and I normally didn't tell on each other—that's why.

I watched as Nan, Felix, and Mom climbed the round oak staircase up to Elizabeth's room.

I listened as the voices grew louder, as a foot stomped down hard and shook the ceiling above me.

I waited for them to come downstairs; they finally did.

Felix looked like he'd been hung out to dry. His shoulders drooped like he couldn't bear the weight of them anymore.

"I didn't know Elizabeth was so in need of her mother," he began. "I'm going . . . well, I'm going to have to figure out what to do about that."

He walked toward his bedroom.

Nan said, "Hildy, it's best to give Elizabeth some space with all this. She's not thinking right now, she's just feeling."

"Laurie liked blue. She was quite an artist," Felix said to my mother at the breakfast table the next morning. He was talking about his wife, Elizabeth's mom.

"I'm sure Elizabeth would like to know that," Mom said encouragingly. "Do you have any of Laurie's drawings?"

"Maybe. I'll have to look later." Felix got up to head to the fields.

"Daddy, wait."

Elizabeth was standing in the doorway in her pajamas. She didn't look at me.

"Morning, honey," he said.

"What kind of blue did Mama like?" Only an artist would ask that.

Felix looked confused. "How many kinds are there?"

Elizabeth sat down as far away from me as possible and ticked them off. "There's azure blue, and teal, and robin's egg, and sky blue, baby blue, midnight, navy, cobalt . . . you know . . ."

Felix didn't know. "Well . . . I'm sure she liked them all."

Elizabeth's face fell.

Felix gulped. "What's your favorite blue, honey?"

"Sky blue," she whispered.

Felix leaned against the back door, relieved; sky blue is something a grower can connect to.

"Well now, it seems to me I remember your mama taking you outside all the time and pointing up to the sky."

"You do?" Elizabeth grinned.

"Yes, ma'am. You two had cloud blue in common."

"That's sky blue, Daddy."

He coughed and headed out the door to the orchard.

"That's a nice memory," I said to Elizabeth, but she wouldn't look at me.

That afternoon at school, Mr. Grasso stood on the stage in the cafeteria flanked by Bobo Liggins and Dave Hargrove, two large, ferocious football players, and announced to one and all the Homecoming Queen winner.

Mr. Grasso shouted, "Lacey Horton, come on up here. You're our new queen!"

A cry of joy rose in the cafeteria as Lacey came forward.

Elizabeth and Jackie sat there shocked.

"*Long live the queen!*" Darrell shouted.

I was standing and clapping next to Zack, who was shouting and whooping.

I looked over at Bonnie Sue's face; it was flushed with fury. The in-crowd girls crowded in around her.

But mostly I was looking at Elizabeth, who was sitting there with Jackie, not clapping, not entering in. I walked over to them.

Jackie's eyes were red. Elizabeth was pressing her temples like she had a headache.

"I'm sorry," I told them.

Elizabeth looked up angrily. "Aren't you going to say you told me so, Hildy?"

"I didn't come over for that. I came over for this." I hugged her. She didn't hug me back much. That was okay for now.

We'd work our way through this.

Chapter 16

✿✿

"Okay, we are going to rock it tonight and we are going to get down and out and over and all around, so get ready!"

Lev shouted it into the DJ's microphone. Lev had painted half his face orange and the other half blue in honor of our school colors, because this, after all, was the homecoming dance.

Orange and blue balloons hung everywhere in the gym. The basketball hoops had been decorated like huge trees with hanging crepe paper apples.

True, the Beasts lost the football game by a field goal, but there was something much more important to celebrate.

The dateless had moved into the seat of power.

True to her word, Lacey Horton had come to the dance alone.

"Everybody dance," Lacey shouted from the stage. "Alone, together, whatever!" She ran to the floor and started a line dance. Pookie, all dressed up in a sequined dog outfit, ran across the dance floor. Elizabeth and her boyfriend, Roddy, did the Electric Slide. Lev did his strutting rooster as people clapped. Tanisha, T.R., Darrell, and I did some swing-dance moves. No one knew if Bonnie Sue was coming. Jackie had stayed home.

The music pounded. I was surprised to see Zack here. He'd told me he hated dances. He seemed paralyzed on the dance floor.

"I don't exactly dance," he whispered to me.

"Can you sway?" I asked him.

"I'm not really a swayer."

"But the universe is always moving, right? Planets in rotation, atoms bouncing around." I danced around him a little. I was wearing my great blue dress from last year. It hugged my hips and had a superb twirling skirt.

He stood there. "Well, actually, atoms move and bond with each other faster than we can imagine—one trillion times faster than the blink of an eye."

"Really?" I blinked my eyes fast and laughed.

"And the atoms we're made of move with us," he added.

"So I'm not just dancing here with myself," I said. "I'm dancing with my atoms." I raised my arms.

Zack looked embarrassed. "I've never thought of science quite this way, Hildy."

Neither had I!

Suddenly, the music changed to a fast Latin beat.

Zack couldn't handle it. "I'm going to stand over there and be inconspicuous."

A hand rested on my shoulder.

"Come on, Hildy. Dance with me."

It was Lev. I shook my head, started walking away. "No . . ."

Lev was already moving to the rumba rhythm. We'd taken salsa dance classes together last year. "Come on."

Kids formed a circle around us, clapping us on.

Oh, why not? I shook back my hair and strutted toward him.

Lev was grinning. My hips were swinging. He twirled me fast and bent me back low.

"See, you can trust me."

Only in public. Back on my feet now.

Lev took my right hand with his left, put his right hand firmly on my back.

I put my left hand on his shoulder; we looked each other in the eye.

"I don't trust guys with blue-and-orange faces," I told him.

He laughed.

Step forward . . .

Step back . . .

Rock forward . . .

Hold the beat . . .

He dipped me back, did a toe-heel swivel.

148

I danced away and danced back to him as the crowd cheered.

I don't know how long we were dancing; my heart was beating fast. Finally the music ended. Everyone applauded. Lev bowed dramatically and kissed my hand. Then he headed to Jenny Johns, his date, who was not amused.

Tanisha came over to me. "You slammed that one, Hildy."

I was glad I had danced with Lev, but I didn't want to dance with him anymore. Now I could honestly say I was over him.

I went to find Zack as the cast of *Desperate People* did a lip sync to "I'm Desperate for You." He was standing at the food table, looking like he'd just seen an alien.

"Hi," I said, breathless.

"Hi."

"Lev and I used to go out," I explained.

"I figured." He put his food plate down.

"Lev and I are over," I assured him.

"Are you sure?"

I watched Lev showing off his lip-synching moves on center stage. "Absolutely."

"I could never dance like that, Hildy."

I smiled. "That's okay. You're an ace at fighting evil."

Zack laughed. "Maybe I should get a cape."

Just then the lip sync ended, and Bonnie Sue Bomgartner paraded in with her date, Bobby Most. She was wearing a hot pink dress and a cold, forced smile. She walked straight to Lacey, clicking off the steps into her stiletto heels. Pookie, ever vigilant, raced to Lacey and jumped up into her arms as Bonnie Sue approached.

Lacey smiled at Bonnie Sue. "I'm glad you came."

"Is this your date?" Bonnie Sue asked sarcastically, indicating Pookie.

"We're just friends," Lacey said warmly.

Pookie yipped and reached out for Bonnie Sue to hold her. Bonnie Sue's face melted as she held Banesville's best little white dog.

Just then thunder boomed outside and fierce rain began to fall, just like the National Weather Service had predicted.

After that, the music started; a slow dance this time.

"Come on," I said to Zack. "This doesn't require much." I took him by the hand, and we walked to the dance floor.

I put my hand on his shoulder. He put his hand on mine and smiled. He was really very cute when he smiled.

"I almost didn't come tonight," he said, swaying briefly.

"I'm glad you did."

I'm glad we all did—dateless and dated.

Lacey glided by, happily dancing with Pookie. They won the dance contest hands down.

Go Beasts!

Chapter 17

❖❖❖❖❖❖❖❖❖❖❖❖❖❖❖❖❖❖❖❖❖❖❖❖❖❖❖❖❖❖❖❖❖❖❖❖❖

MAYOR TO UNVEIL PLAN
TO REVITALIZE BANESVILLE

The Bee reported that a plan that had been months in the making would bring enormous relief to Banesville's lagging tax base. "We need to move into the twenty-first century," Mayor Fudd declared. "We'll be having a Town Hall meeting on November 17 to discuss it. I've never been more excited about what Banesville can give to the world."

I called the mayor's office to ask what that was exactly.

"The mayor will be issuing a statement in the next few days."

The Bee was running a new series of articles about the "run-down orchards on Red Road that were an eyesore," and how revitalizing that land could be good for Banes-ville. They were taking on the high school, too, talking about the fact that fewer kids were getting into good colleges, which, as Zack found out, was true, but only because high school enrollment was down twelve percent.

"You could spin that any way," Zack explained to us at *The Core* staff meeting. "Fewer high school kids are now getting the flu in October because we have fewer kids at the school. Fewer students are taking the SATs, going to the library, getting their hair cut." He dropped his voice like an anchorman: "A new report shows that fewer students at Banesville High School are using the bathrooms, prompting town officials to ask *why?*"

"That's our headline!" Tanisha laughed. "And the photo ops are endless!"

I smiled at Zack. He grinned back.

Halloween was getting closer, but then every day was Halloween in Banesville.

There were reports in *The Bee* about moanings heard by the apple grove on the Ludlow property.

I got a statement from Sheriff Metcalf urging people to be "calm, reasonable, and *restrictive.*" We put that on *The Core*'s front page.

In response, the women's auxiliary decided their annual haunted house fund-raiser wouldn't cause much excitement and they sold mum plants instead.

The PTA cautioned parents to not let their children trick-or-treat.

Madame Zobeck vowed she'd be on Farnsworth Road all night long to commune with the spirits.

"We'll be there, too," promised Pinky Sandusky. The Elders Against Evil were wearing red berets now to go with their team shirts.

"So will we," the sheriff said and he sent a deputy to watch the Ludlow house. Farnsworth Road was closed to visitors and tourists after 10:00 P.M.

Halloween night in Banesville was a nonevent.

But the next day, Lull's Cheap Gas had graffiti spray-painted across the station: DEAR GOD, WHAT'S NEXT?

The Internet site Haunted Houses of New York elevated the Ludlow place from #6 to #1 on its list.

Big tour buses barreled in.

Nothing, it seemed, could stop the fear from growing.

I was at Minska's, an excellent place to be when you're not sure about the cosmos. I wondered what the world would be like by the time I got to be a paid reporter.

I looked at the pictures of Poland's push to freedom.

History repeats itself—I've heard that so often.

"You know propaganda?" Minska asked me.

"Kind of." We'd studied it in history. I sipped my hot caramel chocolate drink. You've got to drink this *slow*.

"Tell me." She crossed her arms across her chest.

"Well, it's . . . it's information put out by certain governments to oppress people."

"Yes, but it's not only the trade of governments." She

walked to the big wooden bookcase against the wall. She opened the case, took out a big dictionary, and handed it to me. I looked up *propaganda*.

The spreading of ideas, information or rumor for the purpose of helping or injuring an institution, a cause, or a person.

Ideas, facts, or allegations spread deliberately to further one's cause or to damage an opposing cause.

Minska walked over to the red SOLIDARITY poster. "Propaganda can happen anyplace," she explained.

"You think it's happening here?" I whispered.

She looked at a copy of *The Bee* on a table. "I believe it is."

"What do we do?"

She smiled. "You know what we learned from living under the rule of Communism?"

"No."

"We learned to get mad."

And she told me how it was when she was twelve. "Those were long days. My mother was working in the underground; my father was in jail. My job was to keep things going on the ground. And I learned that I couldn't do great things, but I could do little things. When people work so hard, when the work is dangerous, you need good food to keep going. So my friends and I learned to cook— I wasn't the best, but I understood how to get food to the workers. I was good at the plan. When I brought the food, I had messages from the others inside—a letter to one, a warning to another, all wrapped in bread or pastry. We used food to get the job done. I used my anger to keep going."

I looked at the photo of hundreds of women pushing against the gate in the shipyards in Poland when the workers' strikes began.

"It must seem boring to you here," I said.

"Oh, revolution can't be forever. But I think it's going to get a bit exciting here. Don't you?"

"Maybe."

"My mother," Minska said, "always told me something when I was going to give up. She said, 'Sometimes just getting up in the morning and standing at the gate can bring the gate down.'"

Home. In my room.

I punched in the phone number for D&B Security. Donald Lupo was dead, Houston Bule was out of jail—I don't know why I kept calling. Obsessive-compulsive issues, probably.

"Yeah, hello?" a woman answered.

I sat up, incredulous. "Is this D&B Security?"

"It used to be."

I tried to clear my mind. "Who am I speaking with?"

"This is Lonnie. Donny's ex-wife."

"Donald Lupo?"

"Not Donald Duck."

Think, Biddle. "I'm sorry about him dying," I said, opening my notepad.

"Yeah, well, he wasn't much of a husband. Look, there's no business here anymore and I gotta—"

I had to keep her talking. "Did he own the company?"

"Donny pretty much was the company."

"Do you know why he was at the Ludlow house so early in the morning, when he died, Lonnie?"

"Martin told him to go. He said it was important."

Martin was the name Houston Bule had mentioned to Judge Forrester. Baker had underlined it in my notes.

"You know, I've been trying to get a hold of Martin . . . ," I said.

"Did you call the office?"

"I don't have the number, Lonnie. Do you?" I closed my eyes. Please have it.

I could hear rustling sounds at her end. "This place is a mess. I don't have it, either," she said.

"So, Donny worked for Martin, is that right?"

"Donny did jobs, you understand? He'd check things out. Look, I've got to lug this stinking furniture out of this office."

"Wait, Lonnie—what's Martin's last name?"

"Geez. I don't remember. He's a big real estate guy."

"In Boston?" I asked.

"Well, yeah. Who are you, anyway?"

What should I tell her? "I'm Hildy."

"Okay, Hildy. Be careful who you get involved with. There's a lotta jerks out there."

I *know.* "Listen, Lonnie, could I talk with you again?"

"Nah, 'cause I move on in life."

I'm writing, I'm trying to think. "Could I just ask you—what kind of jobs did Donny do?"

"You know, I asked him that over the years. He'd say, 'Babe, what you don't know can't hurt you.' Look, I'm outta here."

She hung up.

I wrote, *Babe, what you don't know can't hurt you.*

I'm not sure I agree with that.

Morning. Room 67B.

I could hardly sit still as Baker studied my notes from my conversation with Lonnie. I'd numbered them nice and neat, too—not a crumple anywhere.

"She knew she was talking to a reporter?" Baker asked me.

I looked down and gulped. "Well, there was a slight problem with that and—"

"You didn't tell her?"

"No, because I—"

"Why not?" he demanded.

I closed my eyes. "It all just happened so fast. I wasn't thinking."

He slapped the notes in my hand. "You can't quote her if you didn't tell her."

"But she gave me information!"

"You didn't identify yourself as a reporter, you didn't state your intentions. That's outside the code of ethics. People have a right to know who they're talking to."

"She wouldn't have talked to me!"

"You don't know that."

"But what about reporters who go underground to get a story?" I shouted.

"That's not what you were doing, Biddle."

I slumped in my chair. No, it wasn't.

"What would you have done, Baker?"

"I would have told her there was a great deal of mystery surrounding her ex-husband's death and I was trying to get the facts to be balanced in the reporting."

I wrote that down.

"Tell the sheriff," he added. "See if you can find Martin, the big Boston real estate guy."

I nodded. "I won't not identify myself again, Baker. I'm sorry."

"It's a lesson we all have to learn, kid. Better to learn it early."

After school, I went to see Sheriff Metcalf. He was just pulling his squad car into the parking lot when I drove in.

I got out of the pickup and walked toward him.

"I did something stupid," I told him, "but I might have found a lead."

I told him what Lonnie had told me about Martin and Lupo.

"Boston real estate?" he asked me. "You're sure?"

"Yes. I don't know if she's a reliable source, Sheriff."

"We'll do our best to find out."

Chapter 18

✤✤✤✤✤✤✤✤✤✤✤✤✤✤✤✤✤✤✤✤✤✤✤✤✤✤✤✤✤✤✤✤✤

WHAT'S REALLY GOING ON?

That was *The Core*'s big, fat headline.

Our lead article was Zack's survey. The numbers were in.

Seen a ghost—2 out of 434 respondents said yes.

Heard a ghost—4 out of 434 respondents said yes.

Seen something spooky—10 out of 434 respondents said yes.

Heard something spooky—10 out of 434 respondents said yes.

Witnessed a crime—1 out of 434 respondents said yes.

Committed a crime—0.

Called the police or fire department—3 out of 434 had called.

Wish you'd called (see above)—7 out of 434 wished they had.

Don't get what all the excitement is about—you haven't seen or heard anything—287 out of 434 respondents hadn't seen or heard a thing.

This was way below the town average as reported in *The Bee.*

A new feature, "Let Us Know What You Think," prompted this week's question: *The Ludlow house—scare or scam?*

That got kids talking.

Darrell's feature, "Voices," included twelve letters of protest that had been sent to *The Bee* but were never published. People were writing to us now. "It's time to take the Halloween masks off and see what we're dealing with," Darrell proclaimed in his editorial.

That got the community involved.

Tanisha now had her own page called "Faces," where her photographs of Banesville's residents and visitors were featured.

Overnight *The Core* was hot.

The mayor's office asked for free copies.

I saw Sheriff Metcalf reading the paper in his squad car.

"*All right,*" Baker Polton barked like an Army sergeant. "I want smart reporting from you guys. I want you crawling over every facet of this story like ants on a watermelon."

We can do that!

"Find out what they're doing to combat the graffiti at

Lull's Cheap Gas. Talk to the people who are watching the house. Hildy, I have an assignment for you. I want you to interview Pen Piedmont."

I choked on my unfiltered apple juice. *What?*

"I want you to go over there and ask him two questions—that's all. Where does he think the Ludlow story is going? And where did he work before?"

"You want me to go *there*?"

He nodded and adjusted the photo of his wife and son on his desk.

"Baker," I shouted. "*The Bee* is enemy territory!"

"She'll get ambushed," Tanisha said.

Baker shook his head. "Piedmont's not that stupid."

"But he's powerful!" I said. "He's got more advertising than we've even dreamed about. He's—"

He leaned back in his chair. "Are you telling me you're afraid?"

Yes. But I'd rather not admit it.

"Do you want me to go with you?" He dusted the picture of his ex-wife.

Actually, I want *you* to go, Baker. I'll stay here.

"Hildy's not afraid," Lev assured him.

"That's touching, Radner. You go with her."

"The thing is," Lev muttered, "I . . ."

"I'll go," Zack said quietly.

Baker looked at me with something close to confidence. "Show him how we play the game here."

162

"Okay." I waited for more detail on how we play the game. There wasn't any.

I guess we were making it up as we went along.

Papers piled everywhere.

Phones ringing.

The office of *The Bee* seemed ready to blast into orbit.

"If you want to run an ad," the woman at the front desk said to Zack and me, "we're full up for three weeks."

"Darn," Zack muttered.

I uttered my inane request. "We'd like to interview Mr. Piedmont for our school paper."

"You have an appointment?"

"No."

"He's very busy." She put on lipstick. "And you are . . . ?"

"Hildy Biddle and Zack Coleman from *The Core*," I half whispered.

The woman froze. This ranked among the truly bad ideas of our time.

"Could you see if he has a few minutes?" Zack asked with confidence. If I'd had a paper bag, I would have been blowing into it.

She picked up the phone and told Piedmont we were here. "No, I'm *not* kidding," she added. She pointed toward the windowed office in the back. "He said he's got three minutes."

We walked past a row of desks to Pen Piedmont's office. He motioned us in. His desk was piled high with papers. On the wall was a blowup of the front page with circles drawn around it like a dartboard.

LOCAL GIRL INJURED BY LUDLOW'S GHOST

CROWDS SURGE ONTO FARNSWORTH ROAD

Pen Piedmont threw a dart at the front page. It landed in the ONTO.

"Nice shot," Zack said.

I had my two questions written down in case I was struck dumb by the stupidity of this. Pen Piedmont snarled, "How can I help you?"

I took out my notebook. "Thank you for seeing us, Mr. Piedmont. We'd like to ask you a few questions for our high school paper."

"The high school paper that's questioning the quality of the reporting we are doing here?"

I took a deep breath. "Yes, sir. That's the one."

He looked at me. I didn't look away. He was shorter than I remembered. His thick black glasses were dirty. He put his hands behind his head, bony elbows pointing out. "When you start interviewing other journalists, you haven't got much of a story."

"Mr. Piedmont, you are part of this story, an important part. Where do you think it's going?"

He looked at me like I was an idiot. "You actually want me to tell you where this story is going? You want me to give you information that my reporters have been chasing down for weeks?"

Why did Baker want me to ask that?

"That's not what she meant," Zack said.

But then I got it.

I smiled. "Actually, sir, I'm interested in where *you* think the story is going."

He smirked. "I think it's going big-time is what I think."

I wrote that down. "How so?"

He paused. "Instinct."

Great transition for me. "You've been in this business a long time then?"

"You've got that right."

"Where did you work before?"

His voice changed slightly. He looked at his computer screen. "I started out as a paperboy and worked my way up in various places in the Midwest."

I smiled bigger. "Which papers were you at?"

He waved his hand. "Oh, a few have gone belly up."

A jaw-breaking grin from me. "Which ones, sir? What were the names?"

A cough. "Ah, let's see. *The Des Moines Sentinel, The Green Bay Ledger,*" he said quickly. I wrote those down. I knew he was lying. Lev always talked fast when he was lying.

I said, "Thank you, sir."

"That's all you wanted?"

Zack stretched out his hand. Piedmont shook it. In the corner of his office there was a sign: *The pen is mightier than the sword.*

I went for serious eye contact. "Mr. Piedmont, thank you for your time."

"We're all in this together," he muttered.

Mmmmm . . . maybe not.

Back at school, Zack and I checked on *The Des Moines Sentinel* and *The Green Bay Ledger* and couldn't find anything.

"You're sure that's what he said?" Baker asked.

"Positive."

Baker ran a check, too. The papers never existed. "Call him back and double check," Baker directed.

"But I already asked him and this is what he said. Zack heard it, too!"

"Call him back."

I did. Three times. The receptionist said he couldn't take the call. I told Baker.

"Call back. Say you're on deadline."

"I think he knows that!"

I called back, but no, Pen Piedmont wasn't available.

"Write it up," Baker told me.

"You mean say he lied?"

"Just quote him. That's all you have to do."

As fear grows in Banesville, Pen Piedmont, editor and publisher of The Bee, *said about the story, "I think it's going big-time is what I think." Mr. Piedmont said his "instincts" told him so—instincts developed over the years working from the ground floor up at several newspapers in the Midwest. When asked about which newspapers he worked at, Piedmont remarked, "Oh, a few have gone belly up.* The Des Moines Sentinel, The Green Bay Ledger." *However, after careful checking,* The Core *has discovered that those papers never existed. Mr. Piedmont was unavailable for comment.*

Darrell whooped when he read it.

"Run it," Baker said. "Front page."

If you've never been in print, you don't understand the sheer energy you get seeing your byline, especially when it's on the front page.

Unfortunately, this time my name was misspelled— *Hilly Biddle.*

But *The Core* sold out—sold out, that is, for a freebie, meaning there were no more papers. Mrs. Kutash was strutting around the high school. "That's fine reporting," she said to me.

But Pen Piedmont called it something else.

"Now, I remember when I was in school working at the paper," he wrote in his editorial, "trying to keep up my grades and get out some interesting copy. I think we have to give some slack to inexperienced reporters, but inexperience is no excuse for deliberate misrepresentation, which to my mind is what came out in *The Core*. The pen is a mighty weapon. I offer some advice to the young Hilly Biddle—journalists don't make things up—we leave that to the novelists."

Now it was my turn to throw *The Bee* down.

"I'd be flattered if I were you," Baker told me.

Flattered? "He just insulted me in his Wednesday editorial!"

"He wouldn't have done that if he didn't think you were a threat."

It's between sixth and seventh periods and I have now proved unequivocally that Boston, Massachusetts, has too many people named Martin working there in the real estate business.

Martin Anderson, Martin Cholmsky, Martin DeKalb, Martin Associates, Martin and Sons Real Estate, The Martin Group, Martin Properties, Bimmer and Martin, Robert Martin, Raef Martin, Alexandra Martin-Holdercoff, etc., etc.

Lonnie had called him "a big real estate guy."

That could mean a lot of things—he was successful, he was tall.

I called D&B Security. That number was now disconnected. I tried to find a Lonnie Lupo, an L. Lupo, in the phone directory. All I got was a listing for Lupo the Lion—*children's parties a specialty.*

I tossed my history book into my locker and slammed it shut.

Joleene Jowrey, the lead in *Desperate People*, opened her locker two down from mine.

"How's the desperation coming?" I asked.

She groaned. "Lev keeps going off script, the set is falling apart, Mrs. Terser has become this demon director. All she does is scream."

"I'll be there for opening night."

"Thanks." She headed off.

I stood there trying to get a grip.

"Hildy, can we talk?" I turned around to see Elizabeth.

"Sure."

She took a deep breath and said, "Look, I've been pretty angry at you, but I'm not anymore."

"That's good," I said.

"You can be a total pain, Hildy, but I know you don't mean it."

I laughed. "Sometimes I do."

"But not with me."

"You're right. Not with you."

"So, here." She handed me a plastic bag with peanut butter fudge in it. That's my favorite. It had a little heart-shaped sticker: *Made with love by Elizabeth.*

"How did you know I needed fudge?"

"Everyone needs fudge, Hildy. It's how God helps us cope."

✦✦✦

The fudge was gone when I got the call from Pinky Sandusky the next day, asking me, "How soon can you get to my house?"

Pinky was sitting out back in a green Adirondack rocker, wearing her red Elders Against Evil sweatshirt. She reached down and gave her mutt Lester a biscuit.

"I knew Clarence Ludlow," she began. "He was a cold, calculating man. He told me once he liked the fact that people were afraid of him."

I sat on the rusty bench. "What kind of person would like that?"

"A mean one." She leaned back in her chair and looked across her yard at the last of the red and copper leaves on her trees. The colors of fall were fading now; the leaves were dropping everywhere. "You know the gift of living in town like Banesville?" she asked me. "We learn quick we can't control the weather, but we don't chuck in the towel because of it. We deal with what comes and we figure out a way around the problems."

"That's right," I agreed.

"So we'd better deal with this. My friend lives out on Red Road. Someone came to her house asking if she wanted to sell her family's orchard."

Pinky rocked and rocked, staring at the Ludlow house in the distance. "And this fella said to my friend that he was representing some investors who were interested in her property. They weren't offering a whole lot of money, but she'd better take their offer now because land prices were only going to get lower in that part of town."

I was writing this down, but still watching her face.

"And my friend told him to get his big, honking Cadillac with that Massachusetts license plate off her land, because her great-grandfather had bought and worked that ground and she wasn't selling it."

My brain clicked. Massachusetts—like in Boston?

She stopped rocking and pointed a warning figure at me. "The next day that fella had the gall to come back. He told her, 'Granny, we can do this the easy way or the hard way. It's up to you.'"

"That's awful! Did she tell you his name?"

"I don't think she knew it. The man just barged in." She leaned toward me, hard truth burned in her eyes. "That's what's sneaking in here, Hildy Biddle. Somebody ought to start writing about the real menace."

"Could I talk to your friend, Mrs. Sandusky?"

"I don't know. Right now she's pretty scared."

I walked into the kitchen, got a glass of water, and turned on the little TV on the table.

"It can happen at any time," said the stern-faced anchorman. "Toxic chemicals soaking into the very water we drink."

I looked nervously at my water.

"How sick is your drinking water making you? Stay tuned for a story that could save your life!"

I put the glass down, grabbed my throat.

Mom walked in angrily. "Well, it's official!" She picked up my glass of water, put it to her mouth.

"Don't drink that!" I shouted.

She stared at me. I mentioned the toxic chemicals, the guy on the news. She slammed the glass down.

"The Town Hall meeting about the mayor's plan has been moved up."

"To when?" Nan asked, walking in.

"Tonight!"

"*What?*"

"Tonight," Mom assured us. "And it infuriates me. They're trying to sneak in this meeting so they can say they had it, but keep the crowds away."

"I would imagine," Nan said, "what they're going to be presenting isn't going to thrill all the folks."

Mom took out her cell phone. "Start calling everyone you know. The meeting is at seven P.M. Spread the word!"

Chapter 19

✤✤

Mayor Frank T. Fudd stood in front of the banner made by the Senior Women's Auxiliary, some of whom couldn't see like they used to, which was why the letters were different sizes:

BANESVILLE, NEW YORK
The Happiest Town in the Happy Apple Valley

He looked out at the crowd that had gathered in Town Hall. Not too many of them were happy.

"Well, it's sure good to see so many folks coming out at the last minute." He forced out a smile.

"Didn't give us much choice!" a man shouted from the back.

The mayor wiped sweat from his brow. "I'm sorry about the rescheduling." More people were coming in the side door, so folding chairs were set up. "Without further ado, folks, let's get down to the business of this meeting."

Mom shot up. "I move we wait until everyone is seated!"

"I second that!" someone shouted.

Mom could be a force at town meetings.

The mayor stepped away from the microphone and spoke to a handsome man in an expensive suit. I saw Mr. Grasso in the corner talking to a group of people, Tanisha was taking photos, and Darrell had his tape recorder set up. T.R. and Elizabeth were two rows in front of me. The sheriff was guarding the exit. Nearly every seat was taken now. Mayor Fudd bounded to the microphone.

"This is a meeting about Banesville, friends. This is a meeting about our future. I'm excited, friends. Excited about the future that spreads before us. You know, generations ago, our forefathers came to this land and saw things that needed to be done, and they did them!"

Mayor Fudd could really put a room to sleep. The handsome man in the expensive suit sat there with a Hollywood smile.

"We've got challenges in town," Mayor Fudd continued, "there's no way around it. These last two years of bad harvests have hurt you, hurt our budget, and hurt our future. I'm as resistant to change as the next fella, but you can't survive in this fast-changing world without adapting. And that's what we need to talk about tonight." He nodded to the handsome man who walked toward the microphone. "Now, over the last few months, Midian Associates has been doing an assessment of the best and the worst in Banesville. Mr. Midian is here to present their findings and to offer their suggestions on how we can keep Banesville a force in the twenty-first century. It's not—and hear me well, now—cast in stone. But I've reviewed this and I think they're onto something. So all I ask is that you open your hearts and your minds and let the man talk." The mayor handed the microphone over. "Martin, this is your show now."

Martin?

I dropped my notepad.

Martin turned to us, smiling with bright white teeth. "I'll get right to it, everyone." He had a rich, warm voice. "I want you all to know that in these last few months—my Lord, have I fallen in love with your little town. I'm even a homeowner here now myself. I just bought the Ludlow place up on Farnsworth Road."

A gasp shot through the crowd.

The lights went out.

A big screen to the left of Martin filled with a hazy image that became a 3-D replica of Banesville's downtown.

"Growth," said Martin, "is what the world needs. And how does something grow?" He chuckled. "That's a presumptuous thing to say here in apple country, where you understand the seasons of growth and harvest better than most Americans. But the basics of growth for an orchard are the same as for a town or a city. You've got to have

175

space to grow. You've got to understand what the soil is good for. You've got to prune back the dead leaves on a tree. Growth is only possible when we work at it."

I took notes, even though Darrell was taping this.

More 3-D pictures of Banesville came on the screen and then morphed into a map of the town. Jazz music began to play. "And what's the growth that can happen here? Oh, you can plant more trees. Trees are a fine thing. You can increase the size of your farmers market, spruce up your yards, add a couple of new buildings. But where's the energy of bold new beginnings? The creative thinking that would make Banesville, New York, *the* travel destination in the Northeast?"

People started murmuring.

"What," Martin asked, "could turn this sweet, sleepy town into a mecca of new ideas, bold technology, and good old family togetherness?"

"I bet you're going to tell us, Martin," Mom whispered.

The 3-D map changed into an amusement park with rides and stores. Beyond that were more buildings. "We want to build here," Martin said with feeling. "We want to highlight the mythology of your little apple valley."

The Ludlow house loomed on the screen.

"People are hungry to find new ways to get together. You know the beauty of a theme park? No one goes there alone." A big midway stretched across the screen, filled with families. A dark building cast shadows across the

176

people. "A haunted theme park, ladies and gentlemen, where people can come and find a place to release their fear in a safe environment." A map of Banesville appeared. "It would be perfectly situated along that expanse of badly used land on Red Road. . . ."

Badly used? There were homes there, family farms!

"My great-grandfather bought our plot of land," a man shouted out. "We grow six kinds of apples there, plus peaches and pears. Who are you to say that land is badly used?"

The mayor walked to the microphone. "Now, this isn't the kind of respectful attention I told Martin to expect—"

I heard the sound of a folding chair moving behind me.

"I understand your concern," Martin Midian said gently. "No one's saying you're not using your land, but using it for this new project will bring millions of dollars into this town. Tourism will explode. That means all of you folks who have stores will be riding high. All of you who grow apples will have thousands more customers. The name of Banesville will be known far and wide. Don't you see the beauty of this? Yes, a few will need to be relocated. But the greater good for all will be immeasurable."

Mom stood up. "*Relocated* is a big word, Mr. Midian. Relocated *where*?"

He smiled like a movie star. "That's part of Phase Two. All those issues will be worked out equitably."

A voice rang out. "How can the community take part in this exciting opportunity?"

All turned to look at Pen Piedmont.

"I'm glad you asked that, Pen," the mayor said. "Because we've got a plan to beautify all of Banesville. We're giving a special tax credit to anyone who paints their house up pretty or adds to their garden."

From the row behind me, Baker leaned in close to my ear. "Ask them when the planning assessment report will come out."

I wasn't sure what that was, but I asked it.

"In a couple of weeks," Martin Midian said.

"Ask who gave him the authority to relocate people who have lived on that land for generations," Baker directed.

I asked that, too, and got a cop-out answer about zoning regulations. "We're looking into an equitable relocation package," Midian promised.

"Ask him what research has been done to show how this will affect traffic patterns, crime rates, and pollution," Baker said.

I shouted it across the hall.

Applause broke out.

"Who's that girl asking those questions?" someone asked.

"Why, that's Mitch Biddle's daughter."

That's right.

That's who I am.

The meeting went on for two hours. By the end of it,

Martin Midian had lost some of his tan, but it was clear the Midianite invasion had begun.

I had one more question: "Mr. Midian, where is your company located?"

"We're in Boston," he said proudly.

Chapter 20

The news at school was impossible.

Mrs. Kutash called me into her office.

"Hildy, do you understand how school boards operate?"

"Not really."

"School boards operate on cooperation." She peered at me over her thick glasses. "School boards cooperate with the school and the community. They are comprised of people who understand how the system works."

This sounded bad.

"And I have worked very hard to support *The Core*. But I'm afraid I can no longer do that."

My breath caught in my throat.

"You see, Hildy, based on your reporting, Pen Piedmont is threatening to sue this school."

What?

"And I cannot allow that."

"Why would he sue—"

"He says you have misrepresented the facts about him. He says you have lied in your reporting and fabricated information to damage him by misquoting him about his past employment."

"Mrs. Kutash, I checked everything. I killed myself to get it right!"

"The school board decided that *The Core* must suspend publication until further notice. I have informed Mr. Polton that we no longer need his services."

"That's crazy!"

"What's crazy, young lady, is for the financial security of this school and this school district to be compromised in any way."

"But—"

"There are no buts! I was served a twelve-page summons from his lawyer!"

"Mrs. Kutash, Pen Piedmont is the liar, not me! He uses fear to control people and he's doing that now to get his way."

"I do not give in to fear tactics, but I have to look at the good of the school. We have neither the finances nor the resources to take up this fight. That is all, Hildy."

"Baker Polton was the best thing that ever happened to our paper! There are things going on that—"

"That is all, Hildy!"

That can't be all!

I ran out the door; I couldn't hold the tears back.

I had to find Baker. The bell rang for second period. I didn't care about second period. I didn't care about school boards or cowardly principals or threatening lawyers or any of it!

I ran to Room 67B. Baker was putting his things into a bag.

"You can't go!" I shouted.

"I don't have any choice, Hildy." He wrapped the photo of his ex-wife in paper.

"But we can fight back, right? We don't have to take this!"

We looked at the VERITAS sign hanging crooked on the wall.

He shook his head. "Look, I appreciate how hard you guys have worked. None of this is fair. If you're thinking about doing this for a living, this is decent experience in how lousy things can get."

"Who's going to stand up against Pen Piedmont, Baker? What about Martin Midian and all he wants to do?" I wiped away tears. "Can't we do something?"

"I can't think of anything."

I told the school nurse I was sick. Truer words were never spoken. I was sick right down to my core, sick of the lies, sick of the manipulation, sick of the world that lets bullies keep bullying the little guy until the little guy gives up.

I sat in my truck in the school parking lot, too upset to drive.

182

A flock of birds flew through the sky in V formation. Dad used to say to me they were making a *V* for *victory*.

V for *vanquished* was more like it.

A knock on the window. It was Zack. He climbed into the truck.

"I've been looking for you. I heard what happened."

My hands gripped the wheel.

"This might be the wrong time for me to say this to you, Hildy, but I'm really hoping you won't let this stop you."

"It's over."

"There are other ways to—"

"I quit. *Okay?* I quit reporting." I slammed on the horn. "It's too hard! The rules aren't fair! Don't try to talk me out of it!"

"Okay," he said.

"I'm completely and totally *done*."

"I can hear that."

We sat there in silence.

"I'm probably the wrong person for you to talk to about this," Zack said quietly.

"Why?"

"Well, to begin with, I believe in you."

Bad time to start crying, but I did.

"And the other thing is, Hildy, I don't believe in quitting."

"I guess it's not *scientific*."

"No, it's not. Scientists change the variables until we find the answer."

I glared at him. "I'm out of variables, Zack. The experiment *failed*!"

I wasn't expecting to go to the cemetery. I hadn't been to Dad's grave since spring. Nan came once a week and planted flowers around the headstone. For fall she'd planted ivy and yellow mums.

I was standing there now, looking at my father's headstone.

MITCHELL BIDDLE

That's all it said. I wished we'd thought of something special to put on it. We were all so shocked, no words seemed right.

I sat on the cold ground, remembering the funeral.

The long line of harvest workers driving their trucks in the procession.

MacIntosh running up the center aisle of the church to Dad's casket.

Nan's voice breaking with power and sadness as she closed her eyes and sang "A Mighty Fortress Is Our God."

Uncle Felix weeping—the only time I've ever seen him cry.

Elizabeth handing me a picture of Dad laughing inside a photo frame she'd painted.

Tanisha sitting with me in the silent bond of friendship.

Mom, in the midst of her impossible grief, saying, "I don't know how, but we're going to keep going."

Darrell writing the obituary for the middle school newspaper, calling Dad "a courageous reporter you want to read all the way through." Most people only read the first few paragraphs of a newspaper article.

I touched the grass over his grave.

"I don't know what to do, Dad." I couldn't say any more because I was crying.

My father always knew what to do. In my mind, I could see us walking in the woods together. Dad could find his way back on any trail. It was impossible to get lost with that man. He'd remember bends in the road, landmarks on the horizon.

I felt so lost right now. I felt like everything I'd worked for had died. I touched Dad's headstone. How could a man with so much heart die from a heart attack?

It was getting dark. I hated November. It stole the late afternoon light and brought night too early. I headed to the pickup and drove down the old cemetery road. I could almost hear Gwen, my old therapist, saying, "Hildy, remember, you know how to see in the dark."

I stumbled through the blue door of Minska's Cafe, walked to the counter, and ordered a beef brisket sandwich on an onion roll with creamy horseradish sauce, curly spiced fries, and hot cider.

I ate my food in the back room at one of the round tables. Minska walked to my table and put a piece of her famous apple strudel in front of me. "Free this week for young woman reporters."

"I'm not a reporter anymore." I looked down and told her what happened. "It's over, Minska. All the hard work. The bad guys won." I ate a curly fry in grief.

She considered that. "You want to know something about bad guys?"

I know enough, thanks. I sipped my cider.

"They never win, Hildy. Not really. Come with me."

We walked out the front door, down the steps to the street. Minska stopped at *The Bee*'s corner paper box and frowned with disgust. I saw the headline:

"I CAN'T SLEEP AT NIGHT," LOCAL CHILD CRIES!

"Help me turn it," she said.

"What do you mean?"

She put her hands on the paper box. "Help me."

What was she doing?

"I don't want to see it," she explained. "It gives me a headache. So we turn it."

Inch by inch we turned the heavy metal paper box in protest.

"Okay," Minska said. "That's a start."

186

I followed her back inside the restaurant past the big bookcase, past the couches and chairs in the main room, and into the back with the round tables and the framed photographs of Solidarity's march to acceptance. She stopped at a photo of women standing at a closed gate.

"My mother, she was back here." Minska pointed to a head in the crowd. "She went every day for news of my father. The authorities would give her nothing. They said he was being detained for questioning. They told us this for two years." She turned away from the wall. "They didn't know who they were dealing with. You know who worked day and night to keep Solidarity going?" She watched me steadily. "The *women*."

I gulped.

"Back then in Poland, the Communists didn't see the women as much of a threat, except for a few, like Anna. When they arrested the men, they thought Solidarity would tumble." She laughed. "Women know how to keep the candle burning." She lit a tea light candle on the table. "Yes, we are very good at that."

My heart sped up. "What do you think I should do?" I asked her.

"I think you should celebrate living in a country with a free press."

"I was thinking about retreating, actually."

Minska shook her head. "Not you."

Yeah, me.

"Your school paper is suspended, yes?"

"Yes."

"It sounds perhaps as though you need another one."

What was she saying to me?

"You mean like an underground one?" I whispered.

She surveyed the back room. "We print our own menus here. I suppose we could publish a paper."

"I can't publish a newspaper! I'm only sixteen and I have no idea where to start and I doubt that I even have enough brain cells for this and, honestly, the Polish thing was then and we are here now, and let's not forget that there were thousands of you—"

"Over a million," Minska said.

"Even more reason to quit."

"But it began with one, you see, and then a few joined and a few more." Minska handed me a cup of tea. "You don't understand how much light you've got until the lights go out. My grandmother told me that."

I buried my head in my hands.

"They called the women in the underground press the Dark Circles," she said, "because they didn't get enough sleep; they wrote night and day. When you have something so important, something that you'll stay awake for, something you know that you were designed to do, well, it's worth getting a few dark circles, don't you think?"

Maybe.

"Call your friends. You can't do this alone."

188

✢✢✢

As soon as I got home, I sent the e-mail:

M @ M (Meet at Minska's)

8PM

Back room

Major Need for Silence

On Tanisha's e-mail I added *CODE RED*.

Chapter 21

✥✥✥

Zack, Tanisha, Elizabeth, Lev, T.R., and Darrell sat at the round table in the back room at Minska's, spitting mad about *The Core* shutting down.

"Cop-out Kutash is going to regret this," Darrell shouted. "You know what it's going to be like in this town with only *The Bee* as the newspaper of record? Give me a break!"

"We should get a lawyer," T.R. said.

"You know one who works for free?" Tanisha asked.

"We've been working for free!" T.R. snapped back.

"I think we can be proud of what we've done," Elizabeth said softly. "I think the school is really going to miss us."

Lev balled up a napkin. "Don't count on it."

Zack said, "The thing we've got to remember is that Piedmont wouldn't have threatened us if we didn't threaten him." He turned to me. "So why are we here, Hildy?"

I closed the white window shutters, shut the back door, and laid out the idea for the underground paper, beginning with how just standing at the gate can bring the gate down, and ending with how women kept the candle burning during Solidarity.

Zack laughed. "Can guys be part of this?"

"We're indispensable," Lev said, smirking.

Elizabeth lit a tea candle on the table. "This is just so totally amazing," she whispered, "and I, for one, am way inspired that Minska would think we could even do this."

"We haven't done it yet," Tanisha warned.

"This only works if we're in solidarity," I said. "We don't tell anyone—not our parents, not our dogs. I don't know if Piedmont would try to sue us. I don't know what he'd do."

T.R. nodded. "He had to be desperate to want to sue the school."

I told them what I'd found out about Martin Midian and D&B and their Boston connection.

"So that means Martin Midian could have hired Houston Bule and Lupo to break into the Ludlow house," Darrell said.

"Right," I told him.

"Why?"

"I don't know yet, Darrell."

"But a theory could be that they wanted to make the house seem scarier, right?" Zack asked.

"How do we prove that?"

"Why do we have to prove everything?" Lev sneered.

"We can't print anything we don't know for sure," Tanisha told him. "We've all got to agree on that. If we're not credible, this won't work."

Lev sighed.

"So understanding that," I said, "what do we want the paper to say? What's the purpose of it?"

"To crush Piedmont," Lev said.

Zack's eyebrows furrowed. "It's tempting to do that, but the purpose has to be to educate the public about what's going on. They have a right to know. I think we debate Piedmont with the facts."

Darrell was doodling on his notepad. He looked up. "What's the debate? We've got to define it."

"Banesville is being lied to," I began. "We need to separate fact from hearsay."

"And expose Piedmont as the fearmonger he is," Zack added.

"That's kind of broad," Darrell said. "Can you narrow it down?"

I smiled at him. "You sound like Baker."

"We sure could use Baker now," T.R. complained.

"We haven't got Baker anymore!" Darrell snapped. "It's not fair, but we're it. So let's do the job right."

Lev leaned forward. "Don't you think everyone will know it's us if we put out an underground paper?"

"We just can't admit it," Tanisha warned. "We have to look innocent." She smiled at Elizabeth. "Like her."

Elizabeth beamed.

"Why not do a blog?" Lev persisted.

Zack shook his head. "The readership is too selective. A paper can be distributed to the whole community."

Lev laughed. "Okay, here's our first issue. Hildy interviews the ghost."

"No hype," I said.

"You can't live without hype, Hildy," Lev argued. "Hype is necessary. Nobody will buy anything or read anything if it doesn't promise something big."

I looked across the table. "How many of you say no hype?"

All hands went up except Lev's.

Lev groaned. "Okay, I'll work with it, but as a concept it's got holes."

There were a thousand things to do and only us to do them.

"Has it occurred to anyone," Lev asked, "that we don't have a name for the paper?"

We ate Minska's thin-crust personal pizzas late into the night and brainstormed ideas.

Veritas

The Real News

The Unvarnished Truth

Truth Unlimited
The Oracle
The Voice of Reason
The Real Report
The Banesville Bell
Cored—that was pushing it, but I liked it.

We kept thinking. What *were* we doing on this paper?

"Trying to show what's behind the façade," Tanisha said.

"Peeling away the layers so people can see," Elizabeth added.

"Peeling," I said, playing with the concept. "Pared. Peeled." I laughed out loud. "I've got it, you guys. *The Peel.*"

Elizabeth set to work designing the front page.

"We need to publish," Darrell urged. "Let's go with what we know for sure. It doesn't have to be perfect."

What we had filled only the front and back of a menu-sized sheet.

"I don't think we have enough," I told everyone.

Zack and Tanisha showed the layout to Minska. She held the paper, turned it over. "What's not enough?"

I looked at it. "It's not a newspaper."

"So what am I holding here? It's got news and it's on paper. What else do you need?"

I gulped. "Courage?"

She laughed. "That you've got!"

194

Courage isn't all it's cracked up to be. I always thought it came with some big rush of confidence and adrenaline.

Instead, I just kept moving forward, wondering.

What am I doing?

Is it the right thing?

Would I even recognize the right thing with so little sleep?

Lev, always cocksure, entered full promotional focus.

"Okay, everybody. We're small, we're broke, and we're in way over our heads. But what have we got?"

"Ulcers?" Tanisha offered.

"Clinical depression?" T.R. said.

Lev looked at us with disgust, reached into his shopping bag, and pulled out a vegetable peeler. "We have a symbol!" He gave a peeler to each of us. "Who are we?" he shouted.

We looked at each other.

"Who are we?" Lev demanded.

"The staff of *The Peel*?" I said.

"And what does that mean?"

T.R. leaped up. "It means we're on the cutting edge."

That got Zack standing. "Which means we're on the frontier of progress!"

"We get to the core of things!" Elizabeth added.

"It means," Lev shouted, "that together we can peel them!" He raised his peeler high. "Peel them! Peel them!"

I so didn't want to do this, but T.R. was standing now, slashing his peeler like a light saber, and he, Lev, and Zack were shouting, *"Peel them! Peel them!"* They even got Darrell up and saying it. Guys need rallying cries, I know, but—

Peel them!

Peel them!

Tanisha shrugged and joined in, and Elizabeth followed. I raised my peeler.

Was this how real revolutions began?

"We're going to put posters up all over town late Thursday night so no one can see us," Lev explained. "We're going to put them on the community billboards and in the park. We'll put them on parked cars in driveways. We'll tape them on store windows. Everyone will know and then on Monday the paper will come out."

"Where will the paper be distributed?" Tanisha asked.

"I haven't figured that out yet."

"That would be good to know, Lev."

Zack tapped his peeler on the table. "We can look at traffic patterns in town, get human density factors."

Lev flipped his peeler in the air.

Elizabeth went to work and created a graphic of an apple with the skin peeled partway off to use as our header.

Her design just popped.

I hugged Elizabeth when I saw it. "How come you got all the artistic talent in the family?"

She smiled and looked down.

We printed five hundred fliers and distributed them around town.

GET *THE PEEL*
BANESVILLE'S ALTERNATIVE NEWS SOURCE
PARE DOWN TO THE TRUTH

We were still working on how to get our paper out to the people without being seen.

"We could," T.R. suggested, "just leave them in piles where lots of people go."

"They could get stolen."

"They could also get read."

Zack had identified three key areas—the farmers market, friendly small businesses, and the high school. We compiled a list of the people we would most like to distribute *The Peel*. It ranged from Minska to Lull's Cheap Gas to every farm stand at the market and most kids in the high school.

Everything was clandestine, which, trust me, isn't easy in a small town. We moved from place to place to have our meetings. We wrote at home, e-mailed late at night.

We were constantly getting questions like "You put those posters up, right?" or "You guys are writing the paper, right?"

"We're glad someone's doing it," was how we responded.

"But it's *you*, right?"

And then we smiled and walked away, remembering the First Amendment to the Constitution that protected freedom of speech and the press.

"Does that work for teenagers?" Darrell asked.

I guess we were going to find out.

On November 15, *The Peel* came out on menu-sized paper—it was still warm from Minska's printer when I first held it. Our headline read:

GOOD BUSINESS IN FEAR

The Bee has gone from a 24-page paper to a 64-page paper published three times a week, with special editions. There is good business in fear. The A to Z Convenience Store now has lines outside as people buy Safety First products. More self-help books are selling. Headache and sleep medicine are flying off the shelves in Banesville. The security business is booming. Madame Zobek's psychic storefront is open late into the evenings.

Perhaps you have noticed that Banesville High School's newspaper, *The Core,* is no longer available.

We suggest you ask Pen Piedmont and the Board of Education why.

—The Editors

Six high school kids sworn to secrecy distributed it early Monday morning.

Then we waited.

Chapter 22

❧❧❧❧❧❧❧❧❧❧❧❧❧❧❧❧❧❧❧❧❧❧❧❧❧❧❧❧❧❧❧❧❧❧❧❧

That morning Darrell came to school wearing a fake beard.

"Aren't you taking this a little too far?" I asked him.

"I sense they're on our trail, Hildy. I just want to throw them a little." He pulled the beard down and scratched his lip.

By noon the word was out.

Banesville was half abuzz about *The Peel*.

Between Minska's and Lull's Cheap Gas, we had two places in town where lots of people went and could get the paper. But we needed more.

Thankfully, one thing we needed showed up.

"Well, well," Baker Polton said as he walked into the back room at Minska's. He was carrying a plate of strudel, a mug of coffee, and a copy of *The Peel*.

I was sitting at a window table. The rest of the kids hadn't shown up yet.

Baker sat down. "How have you been, Biddle?"

"Okay."

He looked at *The Peel.* I was dying to know what he thought of it. "How's your writing coming?" he asked.

I didn't make eye contact. "I get to it when I can."

He took off his Yankees cap. "You must have a lot of time on your hands now that *The Core* is kaput."

"Are you serious?" I asked him.

He shook *The Peel* at me. "You want to know the problem with it?"

"*What?*"

"Your writing sounds tired."

"That's probably because *I'm* tired!"

He took out his pen, slashed through my copy, groaning. "Flying off the shelves—you actually wrote that? Have you forgotten everything I've told you?"

He wrote *selling briskly* in the margin.

Whatever.

Baker leaned back. "All that's required to make this a success is for you to write better than you've ever written in your life."

"It's not easy."

"If it were easy, everybody would be lining up to do it!"

"I'm only sixteen, Baker!"

201

"Just don't act like it."

"Are you just going to criticize, or are you volunteering to help?"

He ate his strudel. "I'm just waiting to be asked." Back to my copy. "Explain this piece to me about the mayor."

"He said there was a big meeting at Town Hall in two weeks and he was going to talk about the progress of his plans for the town."

"That's all he said?"

"Yes."

"Next time, stick it in a sidebar. It's an announcement. News would be what the plan is about. Snoop around. See what you can find."

I went to A to Z Convenience to see if Crescent felt like talking.

"I hear you got them running good and scared," she said, stocking the shelf with inhalers, medical masks, and sleeping pills.

I tried to appear normal. "Who's *them*?" I took off my sunglasses so she could see the whites of my eyes.

"All them bees," she said, and turned to nod at the tall, fit man wearing jeans and a nice suede jacket who had just walked into the store.

He touched his earring, looked around. "We can work with this," he said to a woman in a short, tight dress. She nodded and wrote something down on a pad.

Sunglasses off, the man said to Crescent, "Are there other haunted houses around?"

"We just got the one."

"Guess that's all you need." An insincere smile. "We'll be back."

Crescent said she wasn't going anywhere.

The man and the woman headed out the door, climbed into a silver Hummer, and took off.

Crescent put extra-strength headache gel caps front and center. "You catch that?"

"Kind of."

"Keep your eyes open, girl. You know who that was?"

"Who?"

She shook her head. "Now, if I were doing most of the writing, I'd make my way to Farnsworth Road and see what's what." She pushed a business card toward me.

CHAD PRITT

EXECUTIVE PRODUCER

HAIR-RAISING HAUNTS

"THE MOST GHOSTS ON CABLE"

"He's been sniffing around for a while now," she said. "Where you been?"

Doing most of the writing.

I looked at the card. "Do you think this has anything

203

to do with the mayor's plan?" I picked up three Almond Joys, put money on the counter.

"I expect it does," she said, making change.

Now, the problem with being a reporter for an underground paper who is trying not to reveal my identity, even though it seems like half the town knows it, is that if I directly try to interview this guy, I've blown my cover, such as it is, and if I don't reveal myself, I get no story.

I watched Chad Pritt watch the house.

He looked at me, I looked at him, and we both went back to looking at the house.

"We'll need to get the light coming through the trees," Chad Pritt said to the woman in the short dress. "We'll bring Savannah through the gate," he directed. "She can stand on the porch and feel the fear. When they finally move the house, we'll be able to sail in and out of here."

Move the house?

"Who's going to move the house?" I asked him.

"That's not my department," he said dismissively.

Whose department is it?

He studied the house some more. "It will make a great entrance to the park. It's got the gloom and doom we need."

"Sweet," the woman said, writing that down.

"How do you move a house?" I asked Uncle Felix, who was in the kitchen eating low-fat yogurt in abject misery.

Elizabeth was rolling out pie dough. She stared at me like I'd lost my mind.

"How do you move one?" I asked Felix again.

Felix thought about that. "You take it apart and rebuild it, or there's a way to lift it up from the foundation and put it on a flatbed."

"Why would someone want to do that?" I asked.

"Because they're crazy, I suspect." He shoved his glasses low on his nose and peered at me.

"Because they want to preserve the building," Nan offered. She was sprinkling cinnamon sugar on apple slices in a big bowl. "Do you have a particular house in mind, or are you just making conversation?"

I told them what I'd heard.

Felix and Nan looked at each other.

"Where did they want to move the Ludlow house?" Elizabeth asked.

"He said it would make a great entrance to the park."

"You say this was a TV fella?" Felix asked.

"A ghost-TV fella."

"Don't like the sound of that," Nan said.

The cold air had swept in and we were selling hot cider at the farmers market faster than we could pour it. Root vegetables were the order of the day; baskets of baby pumpkins, pears, beans, brussels sprouts, and late fall apples were stacked on tables.

Juan-Carlos worked steadily at our farm stand. He was quieter than usual.

"Everything all right?" I asked him.

"We must talk, my friend. I've been listening for you."

We walked behind the farm stand. Juan-Carlos took off his Biddle Family Orchards cap slowly and pushed back his hair. "I have learned that two workers were offered money to put signs up on the house."

"You mean *the Ludlow house?*"

"Yes."

"Who offered them money?"

"They said it was the man at the paper. Mr. Piedmont."

This was unbelievable. I whispered, "Pen Piedmont is paying people to put up the scary signs at the Ludlow house?"

"Yes." Juan-Carlos looked around to see if anyone was listening in.

"Did they put the signs up?" I asked.

"They refused."

"Would they tell the sheriff about this, Juan-Carlos?"

He shook his head. "These men would never come forward. They need work here. And they have moved to their next job."

Pickers move from place to place to harvest seasonal produce.

"Do you believe what they've said is true?" I asked him.

"I do," he assured me. "They are good men."

"Thank you for telling me," I whispered.

He smiled. "You are much like your father."

I can never hear that too much. We went back to work, but my mind was someplace else.

I had to call Baker.

"I gave you ten dollars," said the customer in front of me. I'd just handed her a twenty-dollar bill back as change, instead of a five.

"Sorry. Thank you!"

I dropped a bottle of apple syrup. I knocked over the change box, too. I dropped to my knees, picking up a sea of quarters.

"Hildy Biddle, you're flapping around here like a wild bird in a cage," Nan told me. "What's going on?"

I gulped. "I need to make a phone call."

"Do us all a favor and make it," Felix grumbled.

I ran out of the stand to call Baker. I found a quiet place near the parking lot.

"I'm not kidding, Baker," I told him on the phone. "I think I've really got Piedmont."

"Write up what you've got on him and Midian."

What's Behind the Haunting?

Martin Midian, the real estate developer who has proposed turning the Red Road properties into a haunted theme park, is going forward with plans to move the Ludlow house to Red Road. What this might mean to the families who live there is unclear.

As the ghostly stories from the Ludlow house dominate the headlines, reliable sources have informed The Peel *that the editor of* The Bee *could be behind some of the mysterious signs that appeared on the Ludlow property over the last few months. This paper is investigating those allegations.*

That got people's attention.

Zack set up an e-mail address for *The Peel.* We gave printed fliers to all local businesses: *Send us an e-mail and we'll get you the paper.*

That got responses.

Good for you.

Count me in.

Nice reporting.

Keep it coming.

But there were others, too.

You kids are going to get caught.

Stop this now.

We know how to find you.

When Elizabeth read the warnings, she got scared. "Hildy, we need to stop!"

"We can't!"

"But look at these. Someone knows we're kids! Someone knows how to find us!"

Baker read them. "What's the sheriff's e-mail?"

Zack found that fast.

"Let's play this safe." Baker replied to the *We know how to find you* e-mail:

> Your message and e-mail address have been for-
> warded to the sheriff's office.

Sweet.

At Banesville High confusion reigned as the administration tried to get information to the student body without
a newspaper. The school's website wasn't sophisticated
enough for weekly postings, and a bulletin board can take
you just so far.

The basketball team didn't get coverage—the only
team at Banesville High that ever won. The canned food
drive wasn't as successful as last year because information
on the drop-off centers was confusing. There were no
faces in the news, no way for feedback, no commentary,
no meeting place to tell our stories.

With no *Core*, there were no interviews with the cast of
Desperate People in the days before their big performance.
There was no opening night coverage, either. Too bad,
too, because in Joleene's big scene when she stormed out
on Lev, the doorknob came off in her hand and she had
to improvise, saying, "Jason, I want you to know that you
can't keep me here. I will find a way out!" And with that,
she climbed through a stage window to huge applause.

In case anyone wants to know what it's like in a community when the newspaper goes away, the good news is
that it's missed. I'd never understood that without news,
people aren't connected.

I was thinking about that as Lev and Joleene stood onstage and brought the final act of *Desperate People* to an end.

"Can this really be all there is to the story of our family, Jason?" Joleene cried. "Can't we learn to be with one another? Can't we learn to be friends, to encourage each other when we're weak and afraid? Oh, Jason, why can't we just learn to make a better world?"

"Your heart shows in everything you do, Monique," Lev responded. "Maybe someday we'll all learn to not be so desperate."

I wasn't taking bets on that.

9 P.M. Minska's back room. The door was closed to the rest of the cafe so no one could see us. Darrell put a printed e-mail on the table.

"It's from a family on Red Road," he explained. "They said they've been threatened because they don't want to sell their land."

"Threatened how?" Tanisha asked.

"It doesn't say. It doesn't have their name either."

We heard Minska shout, "Fire outside!"

We ran out the back door. A fire blazed in the trash receptacle. Zack was yelling for us to stay back. He sprayed the flame with a fire extinguisher, but it didn't do much. The fire department came and got the job done. Thankfully, the fire didn't spread. Tanisha took photos of everything.

Later that night a message appeared in our e-mail:

Keep it up, kids. Next time the fire gets closer.

We sent that to the sheriff, too. It shook everybody, particularly Elizabeth.

"We must be getting close to something if they did this," Elizabeth said. "They know we're kids. They know where we are!"

"No one should be working on this if they don't feel it's right," Tanisha said gently.

"I don't want to quit," Elizabeth whispered, "I just . . ." Her voice trailed off.

"*Look,*" Darrell insisted, "the whole thing has gone too far! Let's give it up, okay?"

Giving up is a grisly concept for Zack. "Aren't we trying to help people not be afraid?" he demanded.

That's when the back door opened. Minska and her husband, Jarek, walked in. "We've been talking," Minska announced. "Here's where we are. The liars and the bullies don't get to do this. We're going to talk to the people we trust to come help us. You do the same."

"Mom!"

I crashed through the kitchen door. I'd been practicing what I'd say.

Look, I've been putting out this newspaper.

I don't regret it.

Sometimes a kid has to do what a kid has to do, and you and Dad always taught me to fight for what I believe in.

Mom was in the living room reading a pamphlet, *Getting the Word Out About Your Fruit.*

I cleared my throat and put a copy of *The Peel* on her lap.

"I've been expecting this," she said.

"You have?"

"Jerry Bass and the rest of the parents have been talking about it."

"*What?*"

Mom pushed her reading glasses onto her head. "Sweetheart, you don't really think that we didn't know?"

"But we hid it."

"From lots of people, I have no doubt." Mom smiled. "I've known you all your life."

I wondered about the other secret agents in the world. Did all their mothers know?

She looked at *The Peel.* "You should be proud of this paper."

"Thanks."

"But I doubt you can sustain it without it taking over."

"We've been noticing that."

I told her about the e-mails and the fire. She got somber then. "You understand, Hildy, that you have to tell the sheriff."

I nodded. "Some of the kids don't want to."

"That's unfortunate."

❖❖❖

"My job," Sheriff Metcalf said, "is to protect the citizens of Banesville, and we've got quite a circus in town."

He looked at the staff of *The Peel* and our mothers; only Darrell was missing—home with a severe headache brought on by consuming fear.

"We've got our local paper getting folks stirred up. I don't like what they're writing. I don't know if you've seen the latest." He opened a copy of *The Bee* and read, *"Courageous reporters use their names. Cowards don't. Truth seekers don't hide. Liars do.* I'll spare you the rest." He paced before us. "But what we've got now has moved into the criminal realm."

A collective gulp. How seriously were we in trouble? Baker came into the room and took a seat.

"Because whoever set that fire," Sheriff Metcalf continued, "broke the law and will be prosecuted to the full extent of the law. And whoever wrote that threat about more fires will have more fires than he or she can handle, I can promise you that." He looked at Baker. "You're part of this group?"

"I advise them."

The sheriff liked that. "You kids might wonder if you've got the right to continue publishing that paper."

"Yes, they do," Baker said.

"That's right." The sheriff walked to the window. "It's my job to protect that right, unless you print inflammatory untruths. I'm not saying you've done that, *but* do we understand one another?"

Yes, sir, we sure do.

"You know," he said quietly. "There are threats to our freedom everywhere. If you kids can figure out how to make things better for people, God bless you. But this is a dangerous road you're on. A lot of people find you threatening. If you're going to keep publishing, I'll give you an official statement that you're being protected by this office. Anyone who steps over that line will be arrested." He tapped his nightstick. "Any questions?"

Elizabeth raised her hand. "I just wanted to say how awesome it's been to hear you talk, and I think I can speak for all of us, Sheriff, when I say that we are very thankful to you for protecting us. Will we have bodyguards?"

"We're not quite set up for that. But with all these mothers, you don't need them."

Chapter 23

❖❖

The envelope was pink, the message written in calligraphy:

> *I have information you will find interesting about the situation in town. Leave a white towel on your front porch railing after 5:00 P.M. if you want to talk. Tell no one.*
>
> *—A concerned citizen*

I couldn't believe it! Someone was contacting me. This could blow this story wide open.

Or it could be a fake.

Even worse, it could be dangerous.

I showed the message to Baker, who half smiled at the calligraphy. "Run it by the sheriff."

I called Sheriff Metcalf, read it to him on the phone.

"A pink envelope doesn't sound too threatening, but you never know. Have you got a white towel?"

❖❖❖

4:37 P.M.

I put a white towel on the front porch railing and looked up and down the street clandestinely. I hoped it was big enough to see; all I had was a hand towel.

My phone rang. It was Zack.

"I need to talk to you," he said gravely. "I need to come over."

"I'm here . . ."

I sat by the window, peering out. A gust of wind knocked my towel onto the ground. I ran outside, put it back in place, and stuck a garden rock onto top of it just in case.

Okay, source, all has been made ready.

The only car that pulled into the driveway was Zack's. He trudged up the steps, looking worried.

"I have to ask you something, Hildy."

"What?" I kept looking out the window.

"I need some help with an experiment. I have this hypothesis and I need to test it. One part I know for sure, the other I don't."

"What are you testing?" I was watching for my source.

He took a deep breath. "Well, here's the thing. I know how I feel about you, Hildy. What I need to know is how you feel about me."

What did he just say?

I turned from the window and looked at him. He scratched his head. He was so cute when he did that.

"I really like you, Hildy. All the data confirms it." He laughed. "And I've been collecting a lot of it."

I grinned. "I really like you, too."

He took my hand; I heard a sound in the driveway. I ran to the window, saw a rear bumper heading down the road. I slapped my hand against the door.

"I can't believe it!" I shouted.

Zack looked at me strangely.

I put my head in my hands.

"Did I say something wrong?" he asked nervously.

"No, no." I took both his hands, told him about the pink envelope and everything.

"If you let go of one of my hands," Zack finally said, "I could put it around your shoulder."

"I can do that."

He moved in close. "I know this is kind of fast," he said.

I laughed. "You call this fast?"

He cleared his throat. "Well, glaciers take centuries."

He kissed me right there, too—a good slow one.

I stepped back, breathless. The best things take time.

Chapter 24

❖❖

Right after Thanksgiving, the mayor's big Town Hall meeting was cancelled. Then anothor pink envelope arrived in my mailbox.

I tore it open to the curlicue writing.

> *I've been sick.*
> *Meet me at Toys "R" Us in the Barbie section*
> *tomorrow at 5:00 P.M.*
> *Come alone.*

I showed it to Baker, who said, "Bring someone with you."

Toys "R" Us. Zack put on a wool cap and sunglasses.

"You look like a bank robber," I observed.

"No toy is safe."

"You go to the Barbies," Zack said. "I'll go to the action toys." He flexed his muscles. "You have your phone if anything goes wrong?"

"I'll probably just scream."

"I'll listen for that." He kissed my nose.

To appear normal, I got a cart and put a Strawberry Shortcake All You Can Be makeup set in it—half off, too.

I walked past the weapons section—handguns, plastic rifles, machine guns, swords, extra bullets. A miserable father stood with his son in front of the model airplanes.

"We can put one together, just you and me, Mikey."

"I don't want one in pieces, Daddy! I want a whole one!"

Not my source. I turned left to the Barbies—rows and rows of them.

"*Psst.*"

I looked around.

"*Psst.*"

"Where are you?" I asked.

"Go to the Fashion Fever Barbie," a woman's voice directed.

"Which one is that?"

"Hair highlights, glam outfit."

I found a Barbie in an iridescent purple dress.

The voice said, "I am standing in the other aisle to not be detected."

"Okay, that's working."

"I have information for you. Are you ready to receive it?"

I took out my pad. "Yes."

"I have information that Pen Piedmont is being paid to write articles about the Ludlow house and the Red Road properties," she said.

Wow. I wrote that down. "Who's paying him?"

"Midian Associates."

I shouted, "How do you know this?"

A child looked at me strangely.

"*Keep* your voice down. I work there, okay? I know what money is going out and coming in." Her voice sounded so familiar—that touch of irritation, that nasal tone.

"You work at Midian Associates?" I asked to clarify.

"I work at *The Bee*."

This was unbelievable! "Do you know why they want him to write these articles?"

"So that the real estate prices would go down and people would want to sell cheap."

My breath caught in my throat. If this was true . . .

"I think they're paying the psychic, too," she said. "That's all I can say for now."

"No, wait. I need to—"

"That's *it*. Don't leave where you are for fifteen minutes. If you do, I won't contact you again."

I stood there waiting. All the Barbies' eyes seemed to be watching me. A man walked down my aisle and eyed the dolls. *That* seemed suspicious.

Then it occurred to me—how would she know if I left? Did she have spies?

"Hildy!"

It was Zack running toward me. "I followed her out," he said.

"You saw her!"

He held up his phone. "I got a photo of her."

"You're a genius."

He smiled intelligently and showed me the picture.

The face was fuzzy but unmistakable. It was Veronica Blitzer, my old babysitter. She always had an obsessive thing for Barbies, too. Zack pressed 411, got the number for *The Bee*, and called it.

"Veronica Blitzer, please. . . . When will she be back? . . ." He wiggled his eyebrows at me and said into the phone, "Who else do I talk to about running an ad? . . . Oh, she doesn't handle ads? . . . Got it. . . . I'll call back." Zack snapped his phone shut and smiled. "It's better than we could imagine."

"What?"

Zack laughed. "It's just so good."

"*What?*"

"She's the bookkeeper. She knows where the money goes."

I grabbed Zack's arm. "Did I mention you were a genius?"

He put his arm around me. "It's always okay to repeat it."

I told Baker what I'd found out. I told the sheriff, too.

"I'm not sure that a bookkeeper would have access to that kind of information," Baker said. "How certain are you this person is on the level?"

"I'm pretty certain."

"Is there any other way you can confirm the information?"

What does he want? A signed confession? "I'm going to lose this story!"

"Before you accuse the local publisher and a real estate tycoon of gross misrepresentation and manipulating the public trust, do yourself a favor, Biddle—make sure you're right."

On Red Road the news was grim. Two more families were about to sell their farms to Midian Associates at painfully low prices. Lacey Horton's family was barely holding on. Lacey told me their phone had been disconnected; they couldn't pay the bill.

Nan had put together one of her blessing baskets for the Hortons, with baked goods, applesauce, and a ham. Zack and I drove to Lacey's house to drop it off.

A black Cadillac was in the driveway when we pulled up. We ran out and headed to the kitchen door. It was open, and through the screen door, we heard a man's gruff voice.

"You'll never survive. You think you're going to sit here in the middle of progress and not sell to us?"

I gave Zack the basket, took out my notepad, and started writing what I heard.

"That's what I aim to do, mister." Was that Lacey's dad talking?

"I'm telling you people once more. This is the best price we're willing to pay for your orchard."

"That's not even close to a fair price, mister!"

"We don't want your house, we don't want your apple trees. We've got bulldozers on the way, pal. I'm telling you now, it's not going to be pleasant around here. We're razing the land we've bought. That's what this is about."

"Get out!" Lacey's dad commanded.

Zack motioned to me and we ran to the side of the house.

We heard the sound of a car pulling fast out of the driveway.

"Massachusetts plates, Hildy. I got the license number."

"Good!"

I could hear a woman crying in the kitchen.

Lacey's dad was shouting, *"Who in God's name do they think they are?"*

"We've got a basket to deliver," Zack said. He took my hand and we walked to the Hortons' back door.

We knocked and walked into the kitchen. Mrs.

Horton and Lacey were sitting at the table. Mr. Horton looked up.

Zack put the basket on the table.

"I heard what happened, Mr. Horton. I hope you're going to call the sheriff. You need protection." I yanked my phone out, offered it to him.

Mrs. Horton said, "I'll get the phone book for the sheriff's office."

"I know the number." I had it on speed dial. I gave Mr. Horton the phone.

"It's going to be all right," I said to them. "We're going to stand together on this."

"Well, well, well," said Baker. "Look what we've got here."

Here was Baker's computer screen. He'd called an old friend at the DMV, who'd quickly traced the Massachusetts license plate on the black Cadillac of the cold-hearted creep who had threatened Lacey and her family.

"Seems the bad guy's car is registered to none other than D&B Security in Boston."

"What?" That's where Houston Bule and Donny Lupo worked. "I thought they'd gone out of business!" I shouted.

"Guess not."

My mind tried to make sense of this. "So that means the creep in the Cadillac doesn't just work for D&B, he works for Midian Associates."

"You've got it, kid," Baker said. "Call your source. Tell her what you already know."

I punched in Veronica Blitzer's number as Baker walked out the door.

After five rings she answered.

"Veronica," I said into the phone, "this is Hildy Biddle."

No sound.

"Veronica?"

A quiet "yes."

"I believe you contacted me because you want to help this town. I need to understand what you know and how you know it. I will never use your name. I promise."

Absolute silence.

"Veronica, please help me."

She took a big breath. "A while ago, I found some holes in *The Bee*'s financial records that didn't make sense—big checks were coming in from Midian for 'advertising' and we'd never run any advertising for Midian—not once. I went to Pen. He said we were publishing advertorials for Midian. That didn't sound right. I started looking deeper."

Their master plan is to turn the Ludlow house along with the Red Road properties into a haunted tourist attraction. In the process, Pen Piedmont, editor and publisher of The Bee, *has been paid twenty-five thousand dollars by Midian Associates to write articles denouncing the state of the properties in addition*

225

to being a partner in the enterprise. Midian hired Donald Lupo and Houston Bule of D&B Security to break into the Ludlow house allegedly to use scare tactics to frighten neighbors, but that plan was stopped when Bule was arrested and, later, Lupo was found dead on the property from a heart attack. Midian Associates also paid Madame Zobek to come to Banesville and con local residents into believing that the ghost of old man Ludlow was present, dangerous, and deadly. The amount Zobek was paid for her part in this corrupt corruption is unconfirmed, a source close to the investigation said. At least three people were paid by Pen Piedmont to put up the frightening signs that appeared on the Ludlow property beginning in the summer.

The strong-armed tactics of Midian Associates were well known among the orchard owners of Red Road. "They sent a big guy to threaten us," one owner recalled. Other orchard owners felt that the safety of their families could be at risk if they did not sell their property at below market prices to Midian.

I wrote and rewrote and checked my notes and ate cinnamon cookies until my sugar level had me on the ceiling. Finally, at 5:00 A.M. I was done.

I sent the article to Baker, leaned over my desk, and fell asleep.

Mom woke me at 8:00 A.M., holding out the phone. "Baker for you."

Reaching for consciousness, I croaked out, "Hi."

"It's great, Biddle. You nailed them."

"Thanks."

"Take out *corrupt corruption*. It's too much."

226

I *liked* that.

"But you're still not done."

I caught my reflection in the mirror—rumpled hair, sallow skin, dark circles. I sure looked done. *Over*done.

"Call Piedmont and Midian. Read the article to them over the phone. Ask them if they have any comments."

That woke me up. *"Are you kidding?"*

"Cover all the bases, kid."

"But I'm clandestine."

"So, you're calling on behalf of *The Peel.* You want to give them a chance to respond."

"But Piedmont has *never* done that for us!"

"That's right. Remind him of how it's done."

Chapter 25

It was a slow morning for crime, and Sheriff Metcalf was eating a glazed apple doughnut when Zack and I walked into his office, holding hands.

"Can I use the phone, Sheriff?" I asked him.

"Are you all right?"

I explained about calling Martin Midian and Pen Piedmont and what I'd discovered. I showed him my article. "I thought I should call from here."

He pressed line three. "Take it at the back desk," he said. "I'll pick up when it starts ringing."

It's easy to be brave when you're writing in a room all by yourself. It's much harder to hold on to courage when you have to confront someone.

Zack put a hand on my shoulder as I tried to reach Martin Midian. He was unavailable for comment.

Suit yourself. I made the next call.

"*The Bee,*" the receptionist answered cheerily.

"Pen Piedmont, please."

"Who's calling?"

I took a deep breath. Time to come out of the shadows. "This is Hildy Biddle calling on behalf of *The Peel*."

She gasped. I heard a click.

"Piedmont."

No turning back now. "Mr. Piedmont, this is Hildy Biddle. *The Peel* is running an article and we wanted to give you the opportunity to respond." No sound on the other line. "Mr. Piedmont . . . ?"

"Read it to me," he snapped.

I did and it wasn't easy, especially since after every sentence he started yelling that it was all a lie and he was going to call his lawyer and if we published that *fiction* he'd bring us down every way he knew how.

I wrote down everything he said. "Is that all you have to say, sir?"

Not exactly. He let loose a string of four-letter words and hung up. I wrote those down, too; my hand was shaking.

If you need to be popular, journalism is not for you.

The sheriff said, "We'll make sure your papers get distributed." He stood up and headed out the door. "I'll be over at *The Bee*. Mr. Piedmont and I are going to have a nice long talk."

We don't know whether the talk was nice or not. We do know that it was long. Pen Piedmont denied everything and accused *The Peel* of libel, which meant we knowingly printed things about him that weren't true. Then Sheriff Metcalf called Martin Midian as *The Peel* came out in full voice. My headline read:

BANESVILLE'S REAL GHOSTS

The sheriff took the papers to the official drop-off centers and guarded them as shopkeepers and other distributors picked them up.

It was a new day, all right.

Piles of unopened *Bee*s were left on the streets for recycling.

Signs in shops sprouted up.

We do not carry The Bee *anymore*.

Proud distributors of The Peel.

The sign at Lull's Cheap Gas was my favorite: *Get Peeled Here*.

Pen Piedmont tried to backpedal, saying that Midian Associates was paying him for "advertising consultation" on the ads they were planning to run for the real estate project.

Madame Zobek declared that ghosts were gathering on the high school property and we'd better watch out!

Zack and I were feeling the rightness of our relationship. I trusted him so much, I told him about how Nathan and Lev had cheated on me.

He held me close. "I can't imagine anyone with a brain wanting any other girlfriend except you."

I was sitting with Zack at Minska's, watching Jarek's cousin lift huge barbells up and down outside. Weightlifters get the point across that a place is heavily guarded.

"Do you like guys like that?" Zack asked quietly.

I took his hand. "I like brainy guys."

"I'd better keep reading then," he said, squeezing my hand.

That's when Madame Zobek walked in. She paused at the door for an extra moment to make sure everyone saw her.

There was a murmur in the restaurant as she slowly moved to a table, raising her hand as a few people said hello. She stopped at one booth, putting her hand to her forehead.

"Your scarf," Madame Zobek said to a woman. "It has been to a sad place."

The woman caught her breath. "I just bought this."

Minska sat Madame Zobek at a table.

"A little water, please, dear one."

The restaurant became very quiet, then a woman's voice rang out: "Did you see that?"

Heads turned to Madame Zobek, whose hand caused a knife to move around the table. That wouldn't have been a big deal if she'd touched the knife. The thing is, she didn't.

"Silly me," she said. "Sometimes the power, you know, just comes out. I cannot help it."

The knife moved just slightly as Madame Zobek's hand hovered over it.

"Science in our everyday lives," Zack said, and headed to her table.

He stood in front of her.

"You are forthright," she said to him. "You have come for information."

"I've got the information," Zack said loudly. "Like poles repel, unlike poles attract." He grabbed Madame Zobek's hand, turned it over, and something from her hand fell out and clinked onto the floor. Zack picked it up, held it high, and announced, "Magnets have remarkable power, ladies and gentlemen."

That's how she moved the knife!

Madame Zobek rose quickly. "I thought this was a friendly place. I sense great darkness here."

"Go figure," Zack said.

She tossed her cape dramatically and left.

"Good friends," Minska said, laughing, "spread the word."

No one knows what the sheriff said when he spoke to Madame Zobek, but the next day she'd left town fast and put a note on her studio door that she had been "called to a new place. The stirrings are strong."

I heard the police had trailed her just outside of Syracuse.

It was like a house of cards falling.

Chad Pritt of *Hair-Raising Haunts* canceled the Ludlow cable TV taping due to "questions of authenticity."

Mrs. Kutash countersued Pen Piedmont on behalf of the school, saying he had knowingly and with malice shut down a "vital school communications network" *(The Core)*.

He denied everything, saying the whole world was out to get him, blah, blah, blah, but even committed liars can't weasel out of everything.

Soon after, he left town on "an extended vacation."

Don't feel the need to hurry back, Pen!

It's a wonderful thing when truth hits the streets. It's like people were starving for real news.

There were smiles—that's the first thing I noticed. Minska said when fear begins to lift, you can see the freedom in people's faces.

Even the early winter vegetables at the farmers market seemed happy. A potato farmer started decorating some of his spuds with smiley faces. Cabbages sprouted eye holes and big toothy grins.

The Elders Against Evil felt the cheer and decided to decorate Farnsworth Road for Christmas with hundreds of blinking lights. They stuck Frosty, Rudolph, and the Holy Family up, too, until a freak lightning storm decapitated Frosty and left the Baby Jesus looking irked.

The big question in town was whether *The Bee* would shut down.

The big question at *The Peel* was, do we fully unveil ourselves and write under our bylines?

233

I talked about it with Mom.

"I wonder, Hildy, how people would have reacted to a teenage paper, really. We adults aren't always the most open-minded when it comes to your age group."

Tell me about it.

"But now I think you're free to let people know who you are."

I went to Minska's to get her opinion.

"The women in the underground press," Minska reminded me, "didn't get the recognition, but they got the results." She handed me the picture of Anna shaking her fist at the Lenin Shipyards. "For you."

"Oh, I couldn't take it, it's—"

"For *you*." Minska tapped the glass over Anna's determined face. "During all the uprisings, everyone knew her name."

I held the photo close.

"What are you going to do now, Hildy?"

I laughed. "I'm going to sleep longer."

"For a little while," Minska said. "And then you take up the next thing."

The next thing came fast and with a fury.

On December 8, Martin Midian held a press conference in Boston.

"We are fully committed to building our haunted village," he declared. "We own the Ludlow estate and several properties along Red Road and will not let challenges stand in our way. We are proud to announce that major construction will begin next week in Banesville, New York."

Behind him was a black banner with white letters:

EVERYONE'S AFRAID OF SOMETHING

The mayor's office was flooded with calls. The poor receptionist kept telling people she didn't know much, but she knew Midian Associates had a permit.

"Is the mayor available?" I demanded on the phone.

"No."

"When will he be available to answer questions?"

Possibly never.

The questions piled higher and deeper.

What about the Hortons' property?

How will this affect Farnsworth Road?

The town?

Our way of life?

Chapter 26

※·∗·※

Dear Orchard Professional,

As part of an exciting community revitalization project, your home and/or land is being purchased by Midian Associates. Because of the blighted condition of your home and/or land, the financial offer is not negotiable. You are required to leave your home and/or land within sixty days of the date of this letter.

Please call 1-888-555-0000 and use your special offer number, 666, to receive your nonnegotiable financial offer and we will put you in touch with one of our relocation specialists. All contracts must be signed within twenty-one days.

We thank you in advance for your cooperation.

Midian Associates

Thinking Today About Tomorrow

I was raging.

How can people lose their land without giving their permission?

"It's called eminent domain, Hildy," Zack said. "It's a law that says a city or community can actually force people to leave their homes if they can prove the land can be used for something better."

"We're not talking about a highway or a hospital, Zack. We're talking about a theme park!"

The mayor's office released a statement: "We believe that the Red Road farmland and the Ludlow property must be put to better use. We support Midian Associates' plans for development and embrace their vision."

Growers stood along Red Road, holding their letters and protesting.

"We're going to raise our voices," Lacey shouted. "And we will be heard!"

Lacey's father painted HELL NO, WE WON'T GO! on their roof.

"Get photos of this," I told Tanisha. "If we have to publish every day, we're going to do it. We're going to make sure everyone knows what this is costing people!"

Zack called our congressman and our senator and was told that the eminent domain law had been approved months ago.

That meant the mayor knew all along.

The Peel pushed out a special edition.

THE GRINCH WHO STOLE CHRISTMAS

For the next two days, we had special one-sheet editions with Tanisha's photos of town angst.

There were meetings at our house about what to do.

A website went up where Red Road orchard owners could get help.

Mom put out a press release.

HAPPY APPLE VALLEY TOWN
ENVELOPED BY FEAR AND GREED

Small orchard owners forced from their land.
And for what purpose?
To build a haunted theme park.

Baker called some friends at other newspapers.

The Elders Against Evil surrounded the mayor's house.

You can tell what trees are made of when the big storms hit.

Lev wasn't helping at the paper as much because he thought a haunted theme park was cool.

"They've hired *the* interactive theme park ride designers," he told me, "and they're going to create this ride that lets people control their own experiences by how they deal with fear."

"You know how I deal with fear, Lev? I don't give into it. I fight it."

"I can sympathize with both sides, Hildy."

"So you think a theme park is worth people losing their land?"

He shrugged. "Well . . . not exactly . . ."

"So you think Midian Associates should be stopped?"

"Well . . . not exactly . . ."

"I think you should turn in your peeler, Lev." He didn't like that much.

"We need people who want to join the fight," I told him.

He pulled me close. "I don't feel like fighting."

"I do." I pushed him away.

The line of construction vehicles wound through town like tanks bringing martial law. They had a job to do—razing the orchards Midian had already bought.

Tanisha, Zack, and I followed behind them in Zack's car. Bennington Orchard was the first farm on Red Road to be leveled—the farmhouse, the barn, and the apple trees—everything would go.

Zack pulled along the side of the road as the trucks thundered up the old driveway. We got out and walked up the drive. This couldn't be happening, could it?

The lead trucker had a steely expression; he was wearing a T-shirt reading BEER, IT'S NOT JUST FOR BREAKFAST ANYMORE. He had a contract he was waving in the sheriff's face that gave him permission to move his trucks in.

The Elders Against Evil raised their fists. They were standing in the driveway looking surly.

"Back those old ladies off," the lead trucker told the sheriff. "They're trespassing."

The Elders Against Evil started booing and hissing.

The sheriff read the contract and walked in slow motion to Pinky and her gang. "You've got to move across the street, ladies. It's the law, but I'm sure not going to have a problem if you take your sweet time."

Two of the elders inched toward the street.

Pinky Sandusky turned to follow and shouted, "My knee!"

I ran up to her. "What's wrong?"

Her eyes were bright. "Why, it's just clicked out on me again, honey. I can't walk. I'm going to have to sit down right here. You help me . . . no, not there . . . *right here on the driveway*." And down she went, holding her SHAME ON YOU! sign.

Suddenly, like a bolt from heaven, the Elders Against Evil were all struck in various aging body parts.

"My hip!" one cried.

"Oh, Lord, my back!" another shouted.

Not to be outdone, Erma Lockeed started shrieking about her "entire lower body going into spasm."

Down they went, helped by Sheriff Metcalf, who turned to the lead trucker and said, "Sorry about this, ace. But we can't move these ladies now. They're going to need medical care."

"They can't stay here!" the trucker shouted.

"Oh, yes they can!" the sheriff shouted back.

Pinky moaned, "I want my doctor."

"What's his name?" the trucker demanded.

"Well, now I'm trying to remember. I can see his face plain as anything!"

The lead trucker flipped open his phone, punched in numbers. "We got a problem, Mr. Midian. Well, it's . . . kind of difficult to explain . . ."

"It's the Elders Against Evil, *hotshot!*" Pinky bellowed.

Tanisha got some of the best pictures of her life that long afternoon, but a sit-in can last just so long.

The ambulance came. Pinky's doctor showed up.

"Go limp, girls!" Pinky hollered, and the EAE went limp in their bodies so it was harder for them to be carried off.

The lead trucker with the BEER shirt watched without compassion. And one by one the elders were taken off the property.

Pinky was the last one to go. "Beer man," she cried, "spare those trees!"

"The area's been cleared," said a man in a hard hat on a walkie-talkie.

And the construction men rumbled their weapons of mass destruction onto the property and leveled that good land to the ground.

We lost two orchards that week.

Meanwhile, at the Ludlow place, construction workers were getting the house ready to move to Red Road.

Niles Van Doren, Midian's architect, came to town to oversee the project.

They dug up the foundation under the house; intersected steel beams across the base; brought in big cylinders with a platform; lined up hydraulic jacks . . .

Day by day our story was appearing in other newspapers.

A David and Goliath Tale, one newspaper called it.

Midianites Strike Again said another.

Fakery Flourishes!

But it didn't matter what we did, what was written, how we protested.

Midian owned the land and they were moving the house.

Period.

DATELINE: Banesville, New York. December 17.

Moving Day. Farnsworth Road.

You'd think God could have sent a blizzard, an ice storm, thick fog, *something* nasty. Instead we got unseasonably warm weather and a happy, shining sun.

A crowd gathered across the street from the old Ludlow house. Mom, Nan, and Uncle Felix stood somberly with Minska and Jarek. *The Peel* staff was here in force.

Elizabeth held a little blue felt flag she'd made that said BELIEVE.

"Believe in what?" Baker demanded.

Elizabeth bit her lip. "Goodness?"

242

Not too much of that on this street.

Zack whispered to me, "You're not taking notes?"

I took out my notepad dutifully and wrote,

thugs in hard hats

2 flatbed trucks—flatbed lowered

steel beams underneath house

<u>*misery*</u>

Tanisha wove in and out of the crowd, taking pictures.

The Elders Against Evil were chanting, "Shame, shame, shame on you!" as Niles Van Doren waved his hand and the two trucks lowered the huge flatbed in front of the Ludlow house side by side. Hydraulic jacks made a screeching sound and began to move.

It would almost have been interesting to watch if it wasn't so awful.

Slowly, the old house was lifted on the steel beams.

I wrote,

the end of an era

the beginning of a new time of—

I was about to write *fear* when I heard a loud sound.

The men in hard hats stepped back.

There was another noise like a giant cracking.

The men in hard hats started shouting.

And before our eyes the Ludlow house cracked—I mean it. Right down the middle!

The porch collapsed; whole walls broke in two; bricks tumbled in the foundation hole; glass shot out sideways.

Construction workers started running toward the street as the house groaned, split in two, and collapsed into itself with a thunderous noise.

Elizabeth gave a little shout and raised her BELIEVE flag high.

I swear to you, I couldn't move.

Zack started laughing and twirled me around as clouds of dust rose into the air.

Baker chuckled, "Stop the presses!"

Niles Van Doren stumbled toward us, a broken person. He fumbled for his phone and put it to his ear.

"Mr. Midian," he stammered, "the house . . . *my God* . . . it collapsed." He sat down on the curb. *"No, sir, I'm not kidding.* The damage . . . is . . . well . . . I'm trying to think of the word. It's in . . ."

"Shambles," Zack said to him.

I kissed Zack in public for that comment as the band of true believers cheered.

The next day, December 18, we got our blizzard.

Snow covered the great mound that used to be the Ludlow house.

Martin Midian's statement was slow in coming: *Midian Associates is assessing the situation.*

Hey, take your time.

Every day people gathered on Farnsworth Road to gawk as one of Banesville's ghosts tried to elbow his way back into the limelight.

Pen Piedmont starting writing editorials. The only kind he knew.

It was old man Ludlow's ghost who broke the house in two.

He's not done making his presence known in town.

He's not going to stop until he takes his next victim.

But no one was listening to that. The Mighty Pen was out of ink.

The Peel came out with our own editorial—*Story time is over, folks.*

The engineering report from Midian Associates said the accident was due to "inherent weakness in the main beams."

The engineering report from the town of Banesville said that Midian Associates were "in too much of a rush to take the time for a full engineering inspection."

"They didn't measure accurately," Zack explained to me. "They didn't have the weight of the house right."

I prefer to think of it as the triumph of the little guy.

Everywhere, little guys were cheering.

The Hortons made it through the winter with a little help from their friends. There was a community Christmas fund set up, and people gave money to help the Red Road farmers keep going.

Midian Associates got such bad press that by March they put the Ludlow property up for sale. The town council passed a referendum that the property could be used only for residential properties. The razed orchards were the saddest sight. They lay there like old battlefields scarred by war. No one knew what would happen to that land.

Bonnie Sue Bomgartner used it as a photo op. She was gearing up for the Produce Princess beauty pageant in nearby Chesterton and taking no prisoners. She stood on the razed ground looking gorgeous and compassionate as a professional photographer clicked away.

It was Zack's idea to plant the garden, not that he was any good at it. He dug a minuscule hole to put the plants in.

"It's got to be deeper," I told him. "The flowers won't take root. The rain will wash them away."

Elizabeth lifted petunias from the starter boxes, knelt down, and started planting a row of flowers near the street on what used to be the Ludlow property. We chose petunias because they're so much tougher than they look.

A little brown rabbit hopped over and smelled the petunias. "Baby animals sense goodness," Elizabeth declared.

"Baby animals get eaten a lot," T.R. mentioned.

But right now we were going symbolic, which isn't always easy for journalists.

I'm standing in the middle of the orchard, trying to appear relaxed as Uncle Felix and Juan-Carlos open the mesh cages and release the bees. It's night and the bees have been sleeping, but now hundreds of them fill the air. This is why I'm wearing mosquito netting over my head—not the greatest fashion statement, I'll grant you. You can say all you want about how bees pollinate apple trees and are a grower's friend. But there's a dark side to bees. If I learned anything this past year, I learned that.

A swarm circles my head.

"Come on, kids," Uncle Felix shouts at the buzzing mass. "Do it for Daddy!"

It takes a minute, but eventually the bees embrace their mission and head for the apple blossoms.

Uncle Felix looks emotionally toward the trees and says what he always says in early May. "If the bees do what they're supposed to do, if the rain holds off, if the wind doesn't blow too hard, if the pickers show up on time and stay with us till the end, then maybe, just maybe, we'll make it."

"We will," I tell him.

"I am certain," Juan-Carlos says with confidence.

Felix watches the bees. "Do you know what your grandfather used to say, Hildy?"

I do, actually. We go through this every year.

"He used to say you could always tell if the harvest was going to be good or bad by how the bees went for the blossoms."

Growers have lots of cute stories to give them hope.

Teenagers are like bees at night, I think. We don't like waking up and we don't always get with the program immediately, but once we figure out our mission, we'll see it through.

Uncle Felix studies the movement of the bees, liking what he sees. "You know, Hildy, I've got a feeling—this just might be a good one."

Special thanks to family and friends for their remarkable support
during the writing and rewriting of this story:
Jean, Tim, Evan, Karen, JoAnn, Rita, Laura, Mickey, Kally,
Chris, Marie, Catrina, Jo Ellen, and Beth.

Much appreciation, as always, to my agent, George Nicholson,
and my editor, Nancy Paulsen.

I owe a debt to four valuable books and their writers:
Pete Hamill's *News Is a Verb* (New York: Ballantine Publishing,
1998); *The Elements of Journalism* by Bill Kovach and Tom
Rosenstiel (New York: Three Rivers Press, Crown Publishing
Group, 2001); *The Culture of Fear* by Barry Glassner
(New York: Basic Books, Perseus Books Group, 1999);
and *Solidarity's Secret* by Shana Penn
(Michigan: The University of Michigan Press, 2005).